LEGENDS
DIAMOND IN THE ROUGH

JEN CALONITA

DISNEP • HYPERION

Los Angeles   New York

For the two youngest Calonitas,
who are both excellent readers.
Gianna and Gio, this one is for you!

First Edition, September 2022
10 9 8 7 6 5 4 3 2 1
FAC-004510-22217
Printed in the United States of America

This book is set in Agmena Pro/Linotype
Designed by Phil T. Buchanan

Library of Congress Control Number: 2022939187
ISBN 978-1-368-04861-3

Reinforced binding
Visit www.DisneyBooks.com

PROLOGUE

12 YEARS AGO . . .

As the last swirls of amber and pink began to fade from a spectacular sunset, a lone horse galloped across the desert.

"Do you see anything?" shouted the man at the reins.

It was hard to hear him over the sound of the wind and the sand flying up around them from the horse's galloping, but the woman knew his question by heart. He'd asked it a hundred times over the last few days as they'd raced across the desert traveling through the mountains to reach their destination. They were out of time, but they kept going. He'd managed to keep them safe this far.

"Nothing!" she told him as she clutched the baby in her arms. The only thing they had to worry about now was the encroaching darkness. "I don't think we're being followed." *Yet*, she didn't add.

"Then we should stop for the night." The man pulled on the horse's reins again and came to a stop. The only sound to be heard for miles was their own breathing and that of the panting horse. "We haven't seen a soul in hours. It should be safe." He touched the silk blanket wrapped around the child in his wife's arms.

"Are you sure? I thought we didn't have far to go," she pressed, staring off into the distance, hoping to suddenly see the lights of a city that could give them safe haven. But all she saw were stars filling the sky as the moon rose overhead.

"Maybe half a day at most?" he guessed. "But it's too far to travel at night." He looked at her with a sad smile. "By tomorrow night, he will be safe. I promise."

The woman nodded. *Safe.* That was what was most important, and yet she couldn't help but feel a pit in her stomach every time she thought about tomorrow.

She was handing her child over to a stranger.

Even after all the discussions they'd had — and they'd had many, most with her pushing for this outcome — she still wasn't a hundred percent certain she was doing the right thing.

Maybe I'm wrong, she thought again. She closed her eyes, praying the visions she'd had while she was pregnant, the ones that haunted her dreams, had been incorrect. *Show me a different future*, she begged the universe.

She exhaled slowly and placed a hand on the child's warm chest. She could feel his heart beating. She let the sound carry her away, her thoughts drifting into a dreamlike state where she could see the vision as clear as a reflection in a rare pool of water. There was her child grown into a strong young man with dark hair and piercing brown eyes running down a sandy path. She smiled for a moment, embracing the sight of the boy laughing as he ran through a stretch of streets, but then the vision changed and her heartbeat quickened. The sand beneath the boy's feet swirled faster and faster, pulling up off the ground and forming a cyclone that slowly morphed into a giant tiger's head with glowing eyes and a menacing snarl.

"Who disturbs my slumber?" the voice in her vision bellowed.

And there was her son heading straight into the tiger's mouth.

What's worse, the next vision she always saw was of her son hanging precariously off the edge of a cliff in the Cave. An old man offers to help him out — if he will hand over the lamp he's found first. *No! Don't give it to him!* she wanted to cry out, but the vision always ended the same way — the precious lamp in the stranger's hands and her son falling to his death, the Cave closing up around him. She opened her eyes, her breath growing rapid and her heart constricting.

For hundreds of years, her family had been part of an elite group known as Diamonds. Their role was to guard the secrets of the Cave of Wonders and its most prized possession — a lamp said to have the power to give its owner three wishes to ask for anything they wanted in the world. A power like that was too big for any one person to possess, and so, like those in her family line that had come before her, she had been tasked with protecting the Cave and anyone who dared try to access it. While this role seemed to come with hardships — Diamonds were constantly on the move, never possessing more than what each of them could carry on their back, their true identity needing to remain hidden in order to protect the Cave — she'd felt a sense of pride and purpose doing this job. And she'd hoped to pass on these lessons to her child as well. She wanted her child to know that being a Diamond was a gift! A complicated gift because while there were several Diamonds tasked with protecting the Cave, only two Diamonds a generation carried the artifact needed to actually open the Cave — a magical beetle that had been split in half for its own protection. Each half had been passed from Diamond to Diamond, moving around the world, in the hopes that the two parts would never reconnect and the Cave would remain closed. This method had worked for hundreds of years, but her visions worried her.

They foretold a different future for her child. One where he fell victim to a powerful sorcerer who would trick him into following his nefarious plan. She suspected this sorcerer was part of the Azalam, a shadowy globe-trotting organization that had long searched for the power to open the Cave to no avail. But if her son gave the beetle to them . . . the Cave would be opened. The fate of the world would be at stake.

This was not a future she could allow to happen.

That's why she needed to get her child to a Diamond who could keep him safe. One whose identity was still hidden from the Azalam. She and her husband had learned that this Diamond's methods were a bit unconventional, but he'd managed to hide other Diamonds before. Once the danger had cleared, they could go back for the boy. But for now, they had to let him go. Keeping him hidden was the child's only hope.

"Wait! Could it be?" the man said suddenly.

She looked over at the man building a fire to keep them warm as the temperature dropped. His large dark eyes flickered in the reflection of the campfire. "Is that Agrabah?"

She squinted to see over the rising smoke and could just make out faint lights in distance across the darkened sky. *Was* that Agrabah? For so long she'd heard about the city's large number of scholars and architectural achievements. Agrabah was a city in which she'd always dreamed of living, raising a family, and learning from the many fine institutions that she wanted her own child to attend. She could see herself in her free time taking up poetry, and studying with those who could help her learn how to be a healer, too. But now that dream was replaced by a new one — one that saw her son delivered safe and sound to his new guardian at all costs. After so many weeks of being on the run, holding secret meetings, and being shuttled from safe house to safe house by stranger after stranger, that was about to happen. Agrabah was within reach.

The babe in her arms stirred and she knew he'd wake and have to eat soon. She just wanted to wait till the fire was roaring and their tent was secure. She lifted the blanket that was wrapped around him and stared down at the child's face as he blinked awake. He had a crop of black hair, thick for a newborn, and even thicker eyebrows, which gave him the distinct look of someone always deep in thought. He looked up at her as she gently stroked one of his hands. The baby wrapped his small fingers around her own, holding tight. Tears streamed down the woman's face.

"Second thoughts?" the man asked quietly.

"A few," she whispered, watching the boy. She looked up at her husband. "What if I'm wrong?"

He placed a hand on her arm that was holding the baby. "Have your visions ever been wrong before?" he asked gently.

No. For once, she wished her gift had betrayed her, but it never had. Since she was small, she had been skilled in reading the stars to gather clues about the future. Her visions were always accurate.

"He'll be safe with him," the man told her again. "He knows what it means to have a mark on his head, just like our son, and he's managed to keep his identity secret from everyone."

"He's said to be reckless," the woman said, unable to keep the bitterness off her tongue.

"He's also said to be the best guide of all the Diamonds," the man replied. "He's unconventional, yes, but smart, and he'll never tell our son the truth about his destiny. Once he's trained the boy, we will come back and tell him ourselves."

The woman had no choice but to agree. As her husband bent down and touched the baby's forehead, the child yawned. The man said something she couldn't hear in the baby's ear, then turned away as the woman snapped the piece of jewelry off her neck and placed it around the baby's. She hesitated giving him this artifact, but she knew it was his destiny to lay hands on it. She could only hope the visions were wrong and the charm would do him no harm. She prayed the Diamond who would mentor him would teach him how to survive in this world with such a price on his head. This charm, in her opinion, was not a gift, but giving him a strong name to carry with him was. She'd already placed a piece of parchment in the baby's blanket with his name on it. A name was an important thing to have and she didn't want him to lose his.

But the necklace . . . to anyone looking for a quick pick, the charm didn't look like much. Tarnished beyond recognition, the gold gem no more resembled a beetle than a rock, and that was a good thing. Hopefully the child would keep the necklace safe, but if it were lost, he wouldn't know what had been taken from him either. In truth, maybe it was even for the best if it disappeared again. The Diamond her son would be with would know what to do.

Her husband placed an arm around her back. "We should sleep."

She looked down at the baby. "I'm not sure I'm ready for the night to be over."

"I know," he said, "but not wanting the dawn to come doesn't stop it from happening." He smiled at her sadly. "Let's enjoy what time we have left."

He was right. She knew he was. She looked down at the baby and wished a million different things for him, but most of all that he would find love in Agrabah, enough to carry him through the harshness of losing his parents.

The baby sighed contentedly and she kissed his cheek. "Good night, our little Aladdin."

ONE

MUKHTARISM NUMBER 22:
BEING AN ODDBALL CAN COME IN HANDY.

"Hey, Lina," Aladdin whispered. "Guess what? The sun will be up soon."

Aladdin didn't expect Lina to answer. Camels didn't talk, of course. But that was okay. Aladdin just needed someone to listen. And Lina, his favorite camel in the entire caravan, was a great listener. Especially when he snuck her some extra grass he'd pulled up before dawn.

"You think it's going to be another hot one? Sunny? Rain? Nah."

Lina gave a bleat and Aladdin kept rambling as he stared at the mountainous ridges in the distance. The faintest traces of light were seeping into the black desert skyline. "Guess we'll soon find out," he whispered, patting the camel's side. "But let's enjoy predawn first, shall we?"

Twilight was Aladdin's favorite time of day. The rest of the nomadic tribe he lived with were still asleep, the camels and goats didn't need tending to, and Aladdin's thoughts were all his own. That's why, the minute he opened his eyes, if the weather was clear and cool, he'd drag his quilted mat out from their tent and find Lina to go look at the stars. The sky was a constant in Aladdin's life. So was Lina, whose birth he had actually witnessed two years before. So in a way, they were family. And he didn't have much in the way of family.

"Where do you think Khalid is going to say we're going next?" Aladdin asked the camel. "Do you think it's west? Or is it east? I can never remember where we head this time of year."

Lina hummed to herself, and Aladdin was certain she was calling for her mother. They usually hummed to each other. Was she bored with his company already?

"Hopefully it's somewhere we can stay longer than a week or two," Aladdin said with a sigh.

At twelve, he'd spent his whole life on the move. He'd been raised by a group of nomadic camel and goat herders who migrated around the desert based on weather and agriculture, finding the best places for their animals to rest. Just when Aladdin would find himself getting used to his surroundings, their elder, Sayed Khalid, would tell them it was time to move on again. Everything Aladdin had to his name, he carried on his back, which wasn't such a bad way to live. You never got attached to material things, or used the money you made to buy ridiculous cymbals at a traveling bazaar. (He'd never done that before. Nope.) A light pack was an easy pack, as far as he was concerned, and he'd rather have room for an extra pillow or a head wrap to ward off the brutal desert sun, than mementos of a place he lived briefly.

"I don't care where we wind up as long as I can still see the stars," Aladdin told the camel.

That was another thing he loved about stars — he didn't have to carry them on his back. And no one owned them. In the caravan, everything one had was shared. Mats to sleep on, water to drink, pillows to rest your head on. (It was a lovely thought, but there was still a part of him that longed for something to call his own.)

But the most important thing Aladdin knew about stars? When in doubt, look to the stars, which are always there to guide you. Elham had taught him that. She was the closest thing Aladdin had to a mother. She'd cared for him after he'd been found alone at a burning campsite. His parents had most likely been killed. All their possessions taken. Elham had said they'd heard his little cries carry over the wind and their caravan had rescued him.

"You are safe in the desert," she always assured him, when he asked about the night he'd been found. "It is those terrible Azalam — bandits that wander the sands hunting for dark magical items — that one needs to worry about. Your poor parents probably didn't even see them coming. But you? The Azalam must have seen that charm of yours and were scared off by the thought that it was there to protect you. Sometimes it pays to be the odd one out."

Odd one out. That was him. A misfit. Even the awful Azalam didn't want him, and he was glad for that, but still, sometimes he wondered if the necklace really did hold some sort of secret he wasn't aware of. The charm was half of something — but half of what he wasn't sure. A beetle, maybe? Why give a baby half a necklace? And a tarnished one at that? "Why do you keep that junk?" someone in the clan would occasionally ask, and Aladdin would jump to the charm's defense.

"This necklace saved my life," he'd say. Elham had said as much. The question was: Why?

Aladdin heard stirring and knew the rest of the camp would soon be awake. Groups slept in large tents held up by a single pillar. While the floor of the tent always looked appealing with its numerous rugs, some good goat's hair mats, and pillows dyed a multitude of colors, Aladdin couldn't shake the feeling that he didn't belong.

"Guess it's time to go to work," Aladdin told Lina as he saw the others emerge and start dismantling the tent. "Today is moving day." Aladdin reached into his sack and pulled out a scarf to keep him cool during the heat of the day. He made sure his necklace was still tied tight around his neck. Then he slipped into the long, multicolored thawb and a sleeveless bisht made of lightweight cotton that the nomads preferred to wear in order to protect their skin from the sun. While the older men and women packed up, he and the other children set out to do their chores with the animals. Goats needed to be milked, hides had to be prepared for trade, and camels like Lina needed to be ready for the long journey ahead.

"Guess I'll start with you, Lina," Aladdin said. "Are you thirsty?"

Aladdin heard laughter and turned around.

Yusuf and Walid were staring at him.

"Tell me you weren't just talking to that camel again." Walid folded his arms across his chest and looked at him oddly.

"He was," Yusuf confirmed.

Aladdin stepped forward, flashing the smile that always won over young mothers, prospective buyers, and even occasionally Amani, the woman who made the tribe's silks. (He'd been known to sweet-talk her into giving him a discarded vest, or to convince her to mend his mended-ten-times-already pants.) "Of course I was talking to that camel. Lina and I understand each other." As if to agree, Lina lifted her head and chewed her food in their faces.

"You're odd, Aladdin," Walid said, shaking his head as he and Yusuf walked off.

They had him there. No matter how hard he tried (and this morning, let's be honest, he wasn't trying), he didn't fit in with the others. They loved to roam, he longed to stay put. They were content playing games, while he was happiest staring at the stars and imagining a life different from his own. His interests were different from Walid and Yusuf's and he never knew how to talk to them. But it was more than that — there was a part of Aladdin that sensed he was meant to be somewhere he'd yet to find. And until he found that special place, he'd always feel restless. He wasn't sure the others would understand that so he only shared these thoughts with Lina.

"I know I should try harder to get along with them, but it's hard," Aladdin said to the camel. He stared off into the desert again. "I'm sure it's because we don't want the same things." He sighed. "I just want to find somewhere I belong and I don't think this is it."

He felt a sharp clap on his back.

"Good morning, Aladdin!"

Aladdin jumped in surprise but was happy to see it was just Sayed Khalid. As the elder of their tribe, he was a man of few words unless there was work to be done. And today there was lots of work to be done.

"Ready for the journey ahead?" Sayed Khalid asked.

"Yes! I'm ready to be on the move again," Aladdin said quickly so Sayed Khalid didn't think he was complaining. "Where are we headed?"

Sayed Khalid smiled. "We are going someplace new. Many tribes have talked about visiting this fine city and now it is our turn. Have you heard of Agrabah?"

"Agra-wha?" Aladdin asked, intrigued. Even Lina stopped chewing and her ears twitched.

"Agrabah," Sayed Khalid said again, sounding excited. The elder loved talking to the children in the tribe about the places he'd visited and things he'd seen on his journeys. He was never happier than he was on moving day.

"Agrabah," Aladdin repeated, the word sticking to his tongue. There was something about the name that made his whole body tingle.

"It's known as a city of opportunity," Sayed Khalid said. "Fine scholars, opportunities to study, marvel at their architectural achievements and science, and . . ."

Go, Aladdin . . . go.

Aladdin looked up at Sayed Khalid as he kept talking. Had he just addressed him? The voice sounded different. Almost hollow like it was being shouted from afar. But there was no one else around but Lina.

"I haven't been there in a long time, but they also have a big market and it's good for trade and their sultan is hospitable."

Go, Aladdin . . . go.

There it was again! Where was that voice coming from? Aladdin looked at Lina, still chewing the last of her grass. Nope, not her. He looked at Sayed Khalid going on about where they were setting up camp and how Agrabah's palace could be seen from every spot in the city. He made mention of sandstorms, but nothing about Aladdin needing to "go" anywhere.

"So you'll have them rounded up and ready to go?" Sayed Khalid asked, and this time Aladdin knew he was being addressed.

Go. Maybe that's what Aladdin heard earlier. His mind was playing tricks on him. "Yes, of course, Sayed Khalid." Aladdin put a hand on Lina, whose backside twitched at his touch. She immediately started to move away, faster than Aladdin had ever seen her. He waved goodbye to Sayed Khalid and ran after the camel. "Wait. Lina! Where are you going?"

Aladdin trailed along after her as she moved toward the other camels in the caravan. "Lina? Come back!"

"Still talking to your camel?" Walid asked as he stood alongside Yusuf. "Telling her all about Agrabah?"

It's time, Aladdin . . . go!

"Who said that?" Aladdin spun around and looked at Walid and Yusuf. "Did you just say 'Aladdin, go'?"

Walid blinked. "No, I just asked if you were still talking to your best friend the camel."

Aladdin . . . it's time!

"There it is again!" Aladdin reached for the charm around his neck. It's what he did anytime he felt unsettled. But this time, the moment he touched the charm, his fingers burned. "Ouch!" He pulled his hand away and stared at his fingertips. They were bright red. He looked down at his charm. It was glowing like a hot ember. "Do you see that? My necklace burned my hand! And that voice? Who is talking to me?"

"Oh, Aladdin," said Walid, walking away. "You're too much."

"No, it's true," Aladdin insisted, reaching for the charm again to prove it. But when he felt the beetle this time, it was cool to the touch. The glow had disappeared, too.

"He's so odd," Yusuf whispered.

Maybe they were right. He was odd. And even worse, now he was hearing voices that weren't there.

TWO ☉

Sayed Khalid was right. Agrabah was amazing.

Aladdin knew it the minute they set up camp outside the city. The city was unbelievable. It seemed to rise up out of nowhere, anchored by a palace of white and gold with rounded domes and finials that almost touched the clouds. He couldn't wait to see the palace up close. He hoped there was time. His favorite thing to do in a new place was explore. There was a part of him — as foolish as it sounded — that was always hoping he'd stumble upon a market or a scent and suddenly he'd know he was truly home. Silly, really, since he'd been with his tribe since he was an infant, but it was still a game he played when he was someplace new. Imagine if home felt like Agrabah's palace? Ha! As if that were possible.

"Aladdin! Stop standing there daydreaming! We have to go set up at the marketplace!" said Elham, who'd already repacked parcels and placed them on camels to take their wares to market. This is what they did in every city and as always Elham had kids in tow to help. She always said it was easier to make a sale when people saw cute kids at the stand.

"Coming!" Aladdin said, taking off at a run to catch up with Lina and a few other camels.

Elham chattered away about what each good cost and what items they were trying to get rid of. (They'd been carrying around the ill-chosen blankets the color of sand for three cities now. People lost sight of the blankets the second they placed them on the ground, so there were a lot of complaints about that item.) Aladdin straightened out his dishdasha, wanting to look his best for the world opening up around him. Then before he knew it, he was inside the city.

"Move along, everyone! We need to get a spot in the marketplace before they're all full!" Elham said as the group moved alongside a large early morning crowd.

Aladdin looked at the tall buildings and numerous streets laid out in front of him and stopped short in awe. The city's gleaming buildings seemed to rise up around him; manicured lawns and groups of people listening to debates seemed to be on every corner. He was so taken with listening to one, he almost got barreled down by a street cart.

"Sorry!" Aladdin jumped out of the way. He walked next to Lina. "Wow," he whispered as much to Lina as himself. "Have you ever seen a place this magnificent?"

Lina sputtered as if to respond.

Each street was more inviting than the last, full of interesting stucco homes, clotheslines with multicolored carpets and garments, and lots of window awnings. Scaffoldings blocked several walkways as construction was under way to build even more buildings. And it was easy to see why. The streets were packed with people of all ages, shapes, and sizes, conversing, playing music, listening to debates or scholars reading from tomes. There were animals everywhere, and vendors aplenty. The smell of samoon and date cookies filled the air.

Performers, families, and guards moved along the streets together as one, and for some reason, that gave Aladdin comfort. He fell in step as he walked along, remarking at how colorful and loud the city was especially as they neared the marketplace.

"Here we are!" Elham said, elbowing her way into a spot next to someone selling fish.

Walid held his nose. "It smells."

"Beggars can't be choosers," she said. "Just hold your nose."

"Excuse me, this is my spot," said a man selling dates and bread on one half of the table.

"Shall we share?" Elham looked at the long table and placed the multicolored cloth she always used for the marketplace (she said it attracted customers) on top of one half. "There's more than enough room for both of us," she said pleasantly, and held out her hand. "Here. A lovely beaded bracelet for your wife." The man hesitated. "Take it. It's important to share the wealth."

Aladdin smiled. "Share the wealth" was something Elham was always stressing to all the children in the Bedouin.

The man looked down at his hand and smiled. "She'll like this. Thank you. Please join me."

"Thank you!" Elham said. She was a master at killing strangers with kindness.

Aladdin's eyes were starting to water, but he painted a smile on his face as Elham detailed all they had to offer — rugs, beaded necklaces, lanterns, and woven baskets the tribe had made.

"Shout out what you have to sell, say it's a bargain and look friendly!" she told Aladdin, Walid, and Yusuf as she immediately got to work herself. Whatever they made today would help buy food to carry them through their next journey . . . wherever that would be.

Aladdin was nudged hard in his side.

"You need to start selling, Aladdin!" hissed Walid. "The sun is already almost overhead."

Aladdin felt tired just thinking about the day he had ahead of him. He could see the day's events clearly — he'd be competing with the others for sales, and it would take him all day to get rid of his items. But if he sold things quickly, maybe he'd have time to see Agrabah's palace. Yeah . . . that sounded like the way to go. Grabbing a fistful of beads, Aladdin stepped away from the table.

"Don't go too far, Aladdin," Elham told him absentmindedly as she worked with a customer who appeared to be interested in one of her gold-woven baskets. "The wind is picking up." She glanced up at a clothesline whipping around in the early morning breeze. "If we have to leave suddenly, I want to know where everyone is."

Walid sighed. "She's always so fearful of sandstorms," he said to Yusuf.

"We haven't been caught in one in forever," he agreed.

"That's because she rushes everyone inside at the first sign of dust in the air," added Walid, and Aladdin quickly stepped away. He didn't want the boys thinking he was eavesdropping.

He also didn't want to admit Walid was right — Elham was paranoid about being caught in a sandstorm, and they hadn't been in one in at least a year. Besides, the weather was clear today and the breeze wasn't anything out of the ordinary. It was just hot air that made one feel even hotter. There was nothing to worry about.

"I'll stay close!" Aladdin yelled to Elham, and gave her a sly wink. "I'm just getting some space to sell so no one cramps my style." Elham laughed. Aladdin stepped away, walking between a vendor making some lamb kebabs that smelled delicious and someone with bread that looked so good, he automatically started to drool. If only he could sell one of these trinkets and buy a loaf. Or some mann al-sama. Would that be so wrong? He stood there for a moment, just staring at the sweet nougat, wishing it would hop into his mouth.

"Tell me you've found the secret entrance! It should be right here!" he heard someone whisper.

Secret entrance? Now, that sounded exciting. Aladdin inched closer to hear this exchange. Most people left him out of conversations, so he'd gotten rather good at eavesdropping.

"Ah, my friend, you know it's not as simple as opening a door," a second voice said, quieter than the first. "Maybe today is not your day."

"But I've been invited inside before!" The first man sounded desperate. His face was cloaked in shadows, a hood over his head obscuring him from view. "You know me!" he railed at a stone wall. "I'm here to make a trade! Let me in!"

Invited where? That's what Aladdin wanted to know. He stepped closer.

"Stop calling attention to yourself. You look like a fool!" said the other man, who was shorter and wider than the first. He wore a royal-blue scarf over his thawb. "The Night Bazaar appears when it wants, to who it wants, and today, my friend, it apparently doesn't want whatever you're selling."

"The Night Bazaar?" Aladdin spoke up, before he could think better of it. "What's that?"

The man removed his hood, giving Aladdin a good look at his face. The man sneered, but it was his eyes that caused Aladdin to pause. He'd never seen gold eyes before. "If you don't already know about the Night Bazaar, then you aren't meant to! Step away, street rat!"

Aladdin stared at the shorter man in surprise. He wasn't sure what a street rat was, but it couldn't be good — weren't rats full of disease and didn't people scream when they saw one? "I'm not a street rat. I'm a vendor!"

The first man shook his head and walked away, but the second put his hand on Aladdin's shoulder. "Don't mind him, my friend. When the Night Bazaar refuses you entrance, it makes one a bit mad."

"So where is this Night Bazaar?" Aladdin looked around. "What do they sell there?"

The man laughed. "Boy, forget you even heard the words. My advice: Don't go looking for something that can't be found unless it wants to be found. It will drive you bananas."

"But what do they sell?" Aladdin pressed.

"It is a place to buy things that the ordinary customer cannot," the man said cryptically. "It's for those who specialize in . . ." He leaned in closer. "Magick properties."

"Magick?" Aladdin stepped back. There was no such thing as magick, was there?

"What do you have here?" the man asked, looking at Aladdin's fistful of beads. "Ahh . . . this blue is my wife's favorite color. I'll take it." The man dropped two coins in Aladdin's other hand before Aladdin could even begin his spiel. Aladdin stared down at his hand in surprise. Two coins! The necklace only cost one, but the man had paid double! For no reason! Elham would be so pleased.

Suddenly a horn sounded, and people stopped shouting out from their stalls and looked up. A crowd was moving through the nearby street, and it grew larger by the second.

"The new grand vizier! He's here!" someone said, and people began pushing and shoving their way over to the caravan, Aladdin being taken along with the crowd before he could even get out of the way. He hopped up and down, trying to see where they were headed, but it was impossible. The crowd was sweeping him away, rows deep and four or five on either side of him. For a moment, he panicked. Where exactly was this crowd going? What if he couldn't find a way back to the market? Elham had told him not to go too far, and now he had no clue where he was. He looked around wildly and saw a girl his own age, her hair in one long braid, pull herself onto a scaffolding near a building being worked on to escape the crowd.

Hey, he thought. *That's not a bad idea.* Quickly, he shuffled sideways through the group of people. "Excuse me! Coming through! Sorry for the intrusion," he said sweetly to a father who had three small children climbing on him. Flashing a bright smile usually got Aladdin far with Elham, so he figured it couldn't hurt here.

"No problem." The man stepped aside.

Aladdin reached the building, grabbed the scaffolding, and jumped. *Oof!* Okay, pulling himself up was not as easy as that girl made it look. He took a deep breath and tried again, this time finally flopping onto the second level like a fish out of water.

"Okay there?" asked the girl with the braid, watching him curiously.

"Yeah." Aladdin jumped up and brushed off his dusty hands, trying not to seem embarrassed at his less than stellar entrance. "Fine. I was just trying to do some exercise before I pulled myself up here."

She narrowed her brown eyes at him. "Exercise, huh?"

"Yep!" Aladdin made what was supposed to be a muscle with his bicep, but sadly there was no bicep to be had. "I climb this ten . . . fifteen times a day actually."

"Uh-huh," she said, sounding unconvinced. "Well, enjoy your exercise."

She took a running leap, and Aladdin let out a tiny yelp as she jumped to a second scaffolding a few feet away. She turned back and looked at him smugly, giving a little shrug, then took off again, jumping to a *third* scaffolding, getting closer and closer to the parade route and the palace without having to deal with the crowds.

How did she do that?

Could *he* do that?

Aladdin took a deep breath. "Well, here goes nothing." He took a running jump, closed his eyes, gave a small scream, and landed on the next scaffolding with a giant *THUD!* His feet weren't ready to stop, though. He skidded to the edge of the second landing. He thought he was about to go over the side. Then he spotted a wooden pole and grabbed on for dear life as the whole structure wobbled.

"Hey!" shouted someone below as debris rained down on his head.

"Sorry!" Aladdin yelled. He had survived the jump and his view was way better! From here he could see people crammed on rooftops and hanging out of windows watching the scene unfolding. He was still pretty far from the palace, if that was the final destination. And where was the girl? When he squinted into the sun, he could see her jumping again. She was already three . . . four . . . *five* scaffoldings ahead of him! It looked like there were scaffoldings all down the street leading to the palace.

"Did it one time," Aladdin said, stepping back to the other edge to start running again. "Bet I can do it againnnnnnnn!" he screamed as he leapt, hitting the third scaffolding a bit more gracefully. Maybe getting cocky was a mistake because when he took off for the fourth scaffolding, he hit it too fast and bounced from the platform into the air. "Aaaah!" Aladdin was flying, arms shooting out wildly, closing his eyes tight, waiting to smack the ground when *BAM!* he hit an awning that broke his fall. He bounced, then rolled off onto two barrels below him, knocking one down. Surprisingly no one even noticed. All eyes were still on the approaching parade.

All but one.

"Nice landing!" said the girl, laughing hard and holding her stomach. "What's your name?"

"Aladdin." He dusted off the dirt on his pant knees and smiled. "And you are?"

She studied him for a moment, her large eyes taking in every inch of him as she twirled her braid in her hand. "Kalila. You don't look familiar." She crossed her arms. "Where do you live?"

"Everywhere" was the truth. He was a Bedouin passing through, but Aladdin suddenly felt a pull — more like a longing — to say he lived right here in Agrabah. He couldn't put his finger on it, but there was something about this city that was calling to him. It wasn't like he was hearing that voice again, but there was a new tingling at the base of his neck that had been there from the moment he stepped inside the city. Why did something tell him his destiny awaited him here? "I'm new to town," he said instead.

"Figured that." She grabbed his arm, giving him no choice but to follow. "Well, you're just in time, Aladdin, to meet our new grand vizier."

THREE

There was no time for Aladdin to argue. He was already deep in the city with no clue how to get back to the market. Was the market even open at that moment? With a grand vizier being announced and a large parade, everyone who was anyone in Agrabah was standing among the spectators to enjoy the show. And he now had a front-row seat to the action. It was still early, and he had sold something for twice its price. He guessed it couldn't hurt to stay a little longer and watch.

"I've never seen anything like this before," Aladdin marveled.

"Neither have I. Grand viziers don't usually put on a spectacle like this," the girl said wryly. "Our last one was always in the marketplace talking to the people, but this guy apparently likes to put on a show."

This was a show, all right. Aladdin could see that already.

"Clear the way!" he heard people shout. "Clear the way!"

From where he and Kalila stood, Aladdin could see half a dozen men in bright garb playing horns as they approached, followed by another half dozen men playing the drums behind them. They were all playing in perfect harmony, and the sound of their instruments together was so loud that some of the children nearby covered their ears. Maybe this new grand vizier was a bit showy, but Aladdin was enthralled. He wanted to hear every sound. Every note. He'd never seen a parade before, and this one seemed to go on forever. Next a group of men and women in bright greens and reds marched by them in succession with flags and billowing capes, followed by more colorfully clothed individuals on a caravan of camels. There were also tumblers and a pack of ostriches and that was all before a massive elephant came into view carrying what had to be the grand vizier.

His turban was larger than the others, his thawb outlined with fine silk and jewelry along with the most outlandish shoes Aladdin had ever seen. He stared out at the crowd with a look of confidence Aladdin knew he didn't possess. He was important and he knew it, even if he was pompous, waving to the crowd with one hand and holding a mirror in the other. Aladdin watched as the grand vizier took peeks at his reflection as they moved down the street.

"Where's this guy from?" Aladdin asked Kalila, looking at the young man's magnificent sartorial display and jewelry. "Must be somewhere really wealthy."

"Not sure," said Kalila. "All I know is he was the first one to answer the call for a new grand vizier. Our last grand vizier disappeared in a storm on his way to a meeting, if you can believe it, and the Sultan has been panicked ever since. He can't work without one."

"He disappeared in a storm? Like a sandstorm?" Aladdin said in surprise. "How?"

She shrugged. "Who knows? All I know is what I've heard through the grapevine and that this grand vizier showed up the week after our old one disappeared, and the Sultan loved him. He made room for him in the palace right away."

"The palace," Aladdin repeated, sounding dreamy. "Living there would be nice."

Up close, the palace looked even more spectacular than before, and all Aladdin could see was through the gates. The parade stopped in front of them, the party continuing while the grand vizier atop his elephant waved to the people as if he were sultan himself. The Sultan didn't seem to mind. Aladdin could see him watching from the second floor, and even he looked excited by the grand vizier's arrival. He was a short portly man with a white beard and bushy black eyebrows dressed all in white with a tall blue feather in his turban. He kept gesturing to a girl petting a large orange-and-white cat beside her.

Aladdin nudged Kalila. "Is that a tiger?"

"Yep! It's Princess Jasmine's pet, if you can believe it," Kalila told him.

The girl, swathed in a blue dress with a small jeweled crown adorning her head, looked unbelievably bored, which he was sure he would not be if he were standing next to a tiger. He was pretty sure he'd be panicked. (Not that he'd admit that to anyone.)

"With any luck, she'll get her father to change the marriage law and will wind up becoming sultana someday," Kalila said proudly.

Sultana, huh? Living in a palace? Someday ruling the city? That sounded like a nice future. What did the princess have to be bored about? Girls. He just didn't understand them.

"And now the new grand vizier will speak to the people of Agrabah!" announced a crier.

A hush fell over the crowd as the elephant slowly moved to the center of the street.

"Good people of Agrabah," said the grand vizier. "I am humbled by your offer to serve this great kingdom!" The crowd cheered. "It is my hope to serve this city well and meet the people who live within its walls!" The people roared louder.

He held his hand up to the crowd to wave and Aladdin gasped. The charm on the grand vizier's necklace! It was a large gold beetle — half a beetle, actually — which looked strangely like the tarnished one around his own neck. Just in much better condition. Aladdin's hand instinctively went to his neck and he clutched the charm in surprise.

BOOM! A giant gust of wind blew through the street, sending the scaffolding swaying. Below, people seemed to lose their balance and a few screamed in surprise, but that was nothing compared to what Aladdin was feeling. His heart was pounding so loud, he was sure Kalila could hear it. Had touching his necklace caused all this to happen?

"What was that?" Kalila said worriedly as she began to climb down the scaffolding.

Aladdin followed, his hands shaky. "I don't know," he admitted.

Aladdin looked at the grand vizier again. He seemed just as bewildered as Aladdin was as he motioned to some of his guards, yelling to them to spread out in search of something. But Aladdin couldn't hear what that something was because soon the horns sounded again and the parade began to break up. Aladdin didn't move. He couldn't take his eyes off the grand vizier's necklace. Did they each have half of the same charm? How could that be? Aladdin boldly took a step toward the grand vizier's caravan to find out when he was stopped by a high-pitched screech.

A monkey was jumping from one person's back to the next. People seemed intrigued until the animal snatched a velvet bag off a man's waist and leapt away again.

"That monkey has my money! You get back here!" the man shouted, chasing after the creature.

"Impressive!" Kalila marveled. "I should give that monkey a job."

"Job?" Aladdin questioned, but before he could ask what she meant, he heard shouting behind him. Some people began moving quickly as the wind started to pick up again. Others pointed to the sky, which Aladdin had just noticed had become almost pinkish in color. Suddenly he had a sinking feeling. People began pushing and shoving to get out of the way.

"Sandstorm." Kalila grimaced. "It looks like a big one."

"Sandstorm?" Aladdin repeated, getting knocked from behind into Kalila. Elham had warned him about the weather and he hadn't listened. He looked around wildly, wondering if he could retrace his steps to make it back to the market quickly. Elham would be so worried if he didn't show up. "How soon?"

He was familiar with sandstorms, having lived in the desert his whole life, but they still made him anxious. When the giant dust cloud rolled in, turning day seemingly into night, Elham had taught Aladdin and the others what to do — run for cover. It wasn't safe to be out in the storm. The sand swirled so hard and fast, a person couldn't escape its foreboding presence (it looked like a thousand clouds moving rapidly at once). Seeking shelter was key. Being out in a storm made it impossible to see or even talk. He had to move fast.

Kalila jumped up on a nearby barrel to try to see. "It's already outside the city. We don't have much time."

Aladdin looked around. He had to find the market. He took two steps to the right, then another to the left. Where was he? How many blocks had he walked and in which direction did he need to go to get back to it fast? People were still jostling him around like the wind soon would. At the palace, flags blew fast in the breeze. The Sultan and his daughter (and her tiger) moved inside as someone opened the gates for the grand vizier and his people to get to shelter. But who was going to take him in? He bit the inside of his cheek. If he couldn't get back to Elham, Walid, and Yusuf in time where would he go?

Kalila reached for his hand. "We have to leave. Are you coming with me?"

Aladdin didn't have to think. He grasped Kalila's hand and ran.

FOUR

The storm was moving in fast. Aladdin could kick himself for not seeing the signs. Elham and Sayed Khalid had taught their whole clan that when the sky turned ashy, the wind picked up, and one looked into the distance and saw a monstrous wall of sand and dust headed their way, the correct response was to run for cover. But Aladdin wasn't with his group. He was currently in Agrabah, where buildings were so tall, he couldn't see the sky unless he looked straight up. Now he'd been caught off guard. Massive clouds were moving in fast as people hurried home, closed up shops, wheeled away peddler carts, and rushed animals inside. As Aladdin and Kalila ran down the street, he could see women covering the windows of their homes with rugs and sheets, trying to do their best to prevent dust and sand from getting inside. Aladdin knew that was almost impossible. (Especially when you lived in a tent like he did.) But one had to try.

"Are you sure your parents will be okay if I wait this out at your home with you?" Aladdin shouted to Kalila. (He had to raise his voice to be heard over everyone else in the streets calling out directions to family, friends, and anyone boarding up their homes.) "This could go on awhile."

"I don't have a mother and father, but Mukhtar won't mind," she said.

Aladdin faltered. So Kalila was an orphan just like he was. "Who's Mukhtar?"

"You'll see soon enough." Kalila flashed him a grin. "Come on! Our place is close by, which means we'll have plenty of time for you to tell me what you're doing in Agrabah!" She took a hard left and hurried down a narrow alleyway. Aladdin watched Kalila's leather babouches kick up dirt as she ran as fast as her feet would carry her. He tried to stick close behind so he didn't lose her in the commotion.

Then he heard screeching. Aladdin stopped short.

A cage holding a small capuchin monkey had toppled alongside an abandoned peddler cart. Crates covered the top of the cage and surrounded it on all sides, making the monkey barely visible, but Aladdin recognized the animal right away. He wore a tiny fez and a purple vest. It was the monkey who had stolen the velvet bag of trinkets in front of the palace. But where was his owner?

The monkey clung to the cage bars, screeching in terror as if he could sense the storm closing in. He was trapped and abandoned. Aladdin couldn't leave him. He turned and headed toward him.

"What are you doing?" Kalila said. "We have to go!"

"That monkey is trapped," Aladdin pointed out, trying to lift the first of the crates that had fallen on top of the monkey's cage. The monkey calmed as Aladdin approached, almost as if he knew Aladdin was trying to help him. Aladdin pushed the first crate aside, and it fell off the cart, rice spilling out of the sides, going everywhere. So that's why the crates were so heavy — they were full of rice. They were going to be impossible to move. "Come help me."

"Aladdin! We're almost out of time!" Kalila yelled. "We can't stop!"

The cloud of dust was moving dangerously closer. Already small particles of dust and dirt were flying through the air feet from where they stood.

"We can't just leave him," Aladdin insisted, grunting as he struggled to move another crate off the top of the cage to get to the monkey. This crate was even heavier than the first.

Aladdin looked at the monkey watching him with big, round eyes. "We're going to get you out of here," he told him.

"You're reckless, you know that?" Kalila said as she stepped onto the overturned cart's wheel and began helping Aladdin push off another crate. The crate cracked open and more rice spilled onto the ground.

Reckless, I'll take it! Aladdin thought. Reckless was way better than odd. He grabbed the crate blocking the monkey's cage door and tried to pull on it, but it was wedged against something. "This one is stuck."

Kalila grunted, trying to pull on the crate, too. "I can't move it and we have to go."

The monkey squeaked and looked at Aladdin again. *No,* Aladdin thought. *I won't leave this little guy behind.* "We can do it, together. On three, we both try to pull the door open. Ready? One, two, three!"

The two yanked on the crate door at the same time and it opened.

"Yes!" Kalila said. "We did it! Now let's go!" The clouds were closing in now, the wind beginning to whip faster.

The monkey looked up at Aladdin with big eyes and blinked unsurely. He was light brown in color, with a skinny body and a long face. "You're safe now, but I have no idea where your owner is and a storm is coming," Aladdin said, talking to the monkey as he would to Lina. The monkey watched him curiously. "Want to come with us?"

The monkey didn't even hesitate. He jumped from the cage to

Aladdin's arm and crawled onto his shoulder as if it were the most comfortable position in the world.

"ALADDIN! Now!" Kalila cried as the dust moved down the street like a river.

"Hang on, monkey!" Aladdin shouted, and he took off after Kalila.

The storm was moving in, making the air so dusty Aladdin had trouble seeing Kalila right in front of him. To make matters worse, the wind made it impossible to hear anything but the monkey's shrieks in his ears. The animal was so freaked out, he placed his paws over Aladdin's eyes at one point and Aladdin had to gently pry them off. He had to focus on the green thawb Kalila was wearing, which was bright enough that part of it was still visible. But for how long? Kalila had said her place was close, but it felt like this journey was taking forever. And part of that was his fault. Just when he thought the sand would overtake them, Kalila cut down another alleyway and began banging on a wooden door, shouting to be heard over the wind. The monkey began to frantically shriek again. The storm was here, rolling down the alley fast.

"Let me in! It's me!" Kalila shouted. If anyone was inside, they hadn't heard them.

Aladdin turned to the door and started pounding, too. No one came.

Kalila and Aladdin looked at each other. There was nowhere left to run.

Aladdin's heart fell as he dared to glance back at the alley. The dust wall was upon them, ready to swallow them whole. He took a deep breath, ready to shield the monkey with his own clothing, when the door flew open and Kalila was yanked inside. Aladdin didn't even have time to shout "Wait!" before Kalila was grabbing his hand and pulling him and the monkey into the darkness along with her.

FIVE

MUKHTARISM NUMBER 1:
PEOPLE CAN'T BUY YOUR TRUST—THEY HAVE TO EARN IT.

Kalila, Aladdin, and the monkey tumbled into the doorway, coughing, the sound of howling wind permeating the room. "Close the door up tight!" someone shouted. "Get those rugs pressed under the door!"

"What were you thinking?" a girl yelled.

"I'm sorry," Kalila sputtered. "I lost track of time."

"You were supposed to be back ages ago," said a boy. "When we couldn't find you, we thought something happened to you."

"We didn't think you'd be foolish enough to be out in a sandstorm!" said the girl.

"I know, I know," Kalila choked out, dry-heaving from the sand.

The little monkey was doing the same. Aladdin couldn't even open his eyes to see what was going on. It felt like he had a million pebbles in his eyes.

"Pitiful," the girl said with a sigh. "Quick! Get them wet cloths so they can clean their faces!"

Aladdin heard the two rushing around, pots clattering before he felt something cool pressed to his face. He held the rag to his eyes and felt his breathing slow. He could still hear Kalila coughing. The monkey kept sneezing, but both were doing it a lot less.

"Thank you," Aladdin said, finally able to look at the boy and girl staring at him. They were around the same age he was.

"You're welcome," said the girl, folding her arms across her chest. Now that his vision was getting clearer, he could see she was taller than everyone else. Maybe she was a bit older, too. "Now, who are you and what are you doing here?"

"Fatima, don't be rude!" Kalila scolded. "His name is Aladdin, and he had nowhere to go, so I told him to come with me. How was I to know he'd almost get us killed trying to save a monkey?"

The monkey started screeching defiantly.

"It's like he's trying to talk to you," said Aladdin, with a laugh. "More like yell at you like a parent would."

"There are no parents here," said the other boy. He was the same height as Aladdin but stockier, with long, dark hair he wore in a ponytail. "Hi. I'm Malik, by the way. My parents sent me to work for Mukhtar when I was five to help put food on the table. And Fatima has none."

Fatima glared at him.

"I don't either," said Kalila. "Although Mukhtar is technically a cousin, so I guess that makes him sort of in charge of me." She smirked. "So he thinks. Like Fatima does because she's two years older."

"It makes a difference," Fatima insisted, and looked at Kalila again. "I was smart enough to get back here when I saw the sandstorm coming. You wouldn't catch me stopping to save a monkey and some kid."

"I'm not staying," Aladdin said hurriedly. "I have a family to get back to. I'm part of a Bedouin tribe. We were passing through Agrabah to sell some goods at the market, and I got separated from the group." Okay, more like he walked off to see the city, but he didn't have to tell her that. He'd learned long ago from Walid and Yusuf that it was better he kept some details to himself. "I just needed a place to ride out this storm. So did the monkey."

The monkey screeched even louder now, raising his paws at the group.

"Let's calm down," said Aladdin, shushing him. "I'm thinking calling you *monkey* has offended you. Am I right?"

The monkey seemed to quiet.

"Then we need to give you a name."

"A name?" Fatima rolled her brown eyes. "He's a monkey."

"A name is an important thing to have." Aladdin scratched his chin, which was still covered in sand, and the monkey screeched in agreement, acting like an elder would — very much in command. Kind of like a parent, or a father. That gave Aladdin an idea. "What do you think of Abu?" he asked, as *Abu* did mean "father of."

The monkey broke into a grin and clapped his hands.

"You like that? Abu it is!" Aladdin said, and gave the monkey a high five.

"Great. Now that we've named the monkey, can we get back to you almost getting Kalila killed?" Fatima growled, playing with the ends of her hair.

Aladdin took in her stony expression and just knew this girl was one you didn't mess with. "Sorry?" he squeaked.

"That's enough, Fatima," said Kalila, placing a hand on the other girl's shoulder. "I'm fine, and hey, this hairy little thief could be someone good to have on our team."

"Thief?" Aladdin asked, looking at sweet little Abu again. "The monkey?"

Kalila, Malik, and Fatima started to laugh.

"Aladdin, didn't you see him during the parade? He grabbed that velvet sack in the crowd, didn't you, Abu?" Kalila cooed. "What did you get? Something magicked?"

"Magicked?" Aladdin wasn't following.

Malik folded his arms across his chest. "Magicked. Kalila, Fatima, and I hunt for items that are out of the ordinary. Special. Magicked. We have the run of the streets near the market. It's our territory."

"Territory?" Aladdin looked around at the room for the first time. The front door was dinged. Piles of rusted loot and cabinets overflowing with intricate vases and jeweled headpieces littered the small space. "What exactly do you guys do with all this junk?"

Malik picked up a rusty candlestick. "I'll have you know we only trade in specialty goods here."

"At least that's what we tell the customers," said Fatima, taking the candlestick from Malik and spitting on it before using her beaded thawb to make the item shine.

"We're technically a junk shop that sells magicked goods," Kalila said. "We work and live here. The more goods we bring in for trade, the better we do. And jewels," she said, looking at Abu, "are even better than a trade. They mean real money and we're saving up to get Mukhtar a bigger place."

"It would be nice to have another room and not have to sleep in the shop every night," Malik piped up.

"Right now, Mukhtar is the only one with a personal living space," Kalila explained. "But if we sell enough magicked items, we can look for a bigger shop. More room, means more items, means more space." She turned to Abu. "So, my furry friend — in exchange for shelter from the storm, what do you have for us?"

"We barely got him out of the cage in time," Aladdin pointed out. "He wasn't carrying a velvet bag. Whatever he had was lost, right, Abu?"

Abu looked from Aladdin back to the other three. With a small sigh, he removed his fez. Two jewels fell from it into his outstretched paw. He grinned, then started to screech again.

Aladdin's jaw dropped. "You hairy little thief. How did you hold on to those?" Abu jumped up and down on his shoulder.

"Nice job, buddy," Kalila said, taking the jewels from him and looking at them with Fatima. "These are pretty decent." She placed them in a clear jar on the table behind her. "Mukhtar will be pleased."

"Who is this Mukhtar anyway?" Aladdin asked.

Kalila looked at Aladdin. "Mukhtar's our boss."

"And our landlord," Fatima said.

"We are a family," Malik added proudly, walking around a large table and banging into a cart, sending two bowls flying. Kalila caught them. "He looks after us and lets us live in the shop."

"Only if you earn your keep."

A shadow appeared in the doorway between the shop's two rooms, causing Abu to screech. Aladdin watched as a tall, lanky man ducked to get through the doorway. His nose was windburned, and he flashed Aladdin a wry smile.

"So, my street rats," he said. "What have you brought home for me today?"

Aladdin stiffened at the term. The men in the marketplace had called him that and it hadn't sounded like an insult. How could it not be? They were being referred to as rats.

"Kalila brought home a person *and* a monkey," Malik said.

"I can see that," Mukhtar said, looking from Aladdin to Abu. "I hope that isn't all you brought me, street rats."

Aladdin's stomach churned at hearing the term again. "Could you stop calling them street rats? These people are your family."

"Doesn't bother me." Malik shrugged. "We are street rats."

"You're better than a rat. We all are!" Aladdin insisted, glaring at the elder in the room, who should know better.

Mukhtar looked at Aladdin curiously. "There's fire in this one." He chuckled. "But the boy is right — you *are* better than rats. Much better." He leaned on a table and stared at Aladdin. "And I don't mean to offend anyone with the term. I refer to myself as a street rat as well. The world outside our door may see rats as scum because they steal things, but in my mind, they're clever scavengers." He motioned to the others. "Just like all of us here. We spend our time on the street collecting magicked items that allow me to own this!" He looked around at the cluttered shop and his eyes gleamed. "So when I say *street rat*, I am playing around with the term. The world sees a thief, but we know better what we truly are."

Aladdin was quiet for a moment, listening to the wind. Now he felt foolish for getting so mad. Mukhtar wasn't being mean, but that didn't mean the words didn't sting. "The term is still offensive, but thanks for explaining."

Mukhtar nodded. "You make a fair point. Maybe I should refer to us as something else. Now, what to call you instead . . ." His fingers drummed the table next to him.

Fatima snorted. "We should charge Mukhtar a coin every time he uses the phrase. That would make him stop." The others laughed.

"I see I have my work cut out for me!" Mukhtar rubbed his hands together. "I'll come up with something, but for now, back to my question: What do you all have for me today?"

Kalila reached into the satchel on her hip. "These bracelets felt like they could be magicked. So did this flute."

"Nice!" Mukhtar turned the items over in his hands. He had long fingers. "Hand-carved," he said. "I feel like we've seen something like this come through the shop before."

"Me next," said Malik, hurrying forward. He dumped out the contents of his silk bag, showing off two oil lamps. "The way they were flickering, it felt like they called to me."

Aladdin held his breath. Did these kids hear voices, too?

"Nice! We will light them and see what happens."

"My score is the best," Fatima said, pushing forward. She dropped three scarves on the table, then pulled a jeweled cuff off her arm.

Kalila, Malik, and Mukhtar leaned in to look at at it. "Oooh!" they said at the same time.

"Yep! I heard the women whispering while she touched the cuff and I thought — magicked! I even drew a picture of the woman who was wearing it." She held out a scrap of parchment with a detailed sketch of a woman in the marketplace.

"Fatima wants to be an illustrator," said Kalila.

Fatima jut out her chin. "And I will be. I'm going to study with the finest illustrators someday."

"You stole all these things?" Aladdin asked.

"We see it as returning the items to their rightful owners," said Kalila matter-of-factly.

"Magicked items deserve to be in their rightful homes," Malik added.

Home. Aladdin let the word sit with him for a minute. It was the one thing he secretly longed for. He immediately felt guilty for wanting one. He knew the tribe loved and cared for him.

"So what about Aladdin here?" Mukhtar turned to him with a dark stare. "Find anything for me?"

"He doesn't know how to find magicked things," Kalila reminded him. "He's just here to get out of the storm."

"Everyone who resides here needs to do their part," Mukhtar reminded her.

Aladdin could hear the storm still raging. The door to the small shop looked like it might blow from the way it was creaking and moaning. Even though every window and door crack had been stuffed with blankets, the candles in the shop still flickered as if they might go out and plunge them into darkness at any moment. He did not want to be out in that storm. He didn't want Abu out there, either. But what did he have to offer? Fatima had already taken Abu's jewels and didn't seem to want to let him take credit for finding them. Did he have anything else valuable?

Well, maybe not valuable, but it was to him. He held up his necklace. "I do have this."

Malik started to laugh. "That tarnished thing?"

"It looks like junk!" Fatima said.

"Guys, be nice," Kalila scolded.

"I know it doesn't look like much, but it's all I have," Aladdin said, taking it off and grabbing a rag on a table to try to clean the charm off. He scrubbed it for a moment, and a section of tarnish cleared, revealing a shiny gold underneath.

Aladdin's heart lurched. If Mukhtar actually took it, he wasn't sure he could bear it. But what choice did he have?

Mukhtar was chuckling, too, till he came in closer and looked at the tarnished beetle swinging from the rope. That's when he promptly stopped laughing and stared from the necklace to Aladdin, his hands pausing in midair inches from the charm. "Where did you get this?" he whispered.

"The junk pile?" Fatima joked.

"Hush!" Mukhtar said sternly, his eyes not leaving the necklace. He slowly turned to Aladdin. "I asked you a question. Where did you get this?"

"Mukhtar," Kalila interrupted, looking uncomfortable. "Are you all right?"

Aladdin didn't understand what was happening. Mukhtar seemed anxious, as if the charm were cursed, and yet he also couldn't take his eyes off it. "It was my mother's," Aladdin explained. "At least that's what the Bedouin told me. They said it wasn't worth much, but it's all I have of hers."

Mukhtar continued to stare. "This was your mother's? You're sure?"

"Yes, sir," Aladdin said, staring down at his leather shoes.

"She gave you this?" he repeated, and Aladdin nodded unsurely. "Where have you both been the last twelve years?"

Aladdin was confused by his reaction. "My mother is gone. And how did you know I was twelve?"

Mukhtar's eyes widened and he grabbed Aladdin suddenly by his shoulders. "How did you get here? How did you find me?"

"Me? He didn't find you, he found me!" Kalila said. "Mukhtar, what has gotten into you?" She looked sheepishly at Aladdin. "He's not normally like this. I'm sorry."

"He only gets this agitated when they run out of knafeh at the market," Malik said with a shrug. "Mukhtar, it's like you've seen a spirit!"

"It can't be . . . but yet . . ." Mukhtar strangely pulled Aladdin into a hug and wouldn't let go. Aladdin was so surprised, he didn't know what to do. Abu cried softly, equally unsure. Mukhtar's laugh turned into a sob as his hands dug deeper into Aladdin's shoulders "I thought you were dead."

Aladdin froze. "Me?" He didn't know who this guy was. Mukhtar clearly had him confused with someone else.

"Mukhtar," Kalila said gently. "Let him go. You're scaring him."

"You're scaring all of us," Malik agreed. "What do you mean you thought Aladdin was dead?"

"You're not making sense — do you two know each other?" Fatima asked, watching them both suspiciously.

"No," Aladdin and Mukhtar said at the same time.

"Forgive me," said Mukhtar, letting Aladdin go and staring everywhere but at him. "I must be seeing things — being cooped up in this storm and all. I need some fresh air." He shook his head. "I'm sorry. I thought you were someone else."

"Who did you think he was?" Kalila pressed.

Abu jumped onto Aladdin's shoulder protectively, and Aladdin felt a familiar tingling at the back of his neck again. He tried to ignore it. Mukhtar had made a mistake. At least his necklace hadn't started to glow.

"Someone whose care was to be placed in my hands a long time ago," Mukhtar said, shifting his body weight slightly.

"Like you do for us, right?" Malik piped up, and looked at Aladdin. "That's how he got stuck with Fatima and me — he likes to take in strays."

Fatima swatted him. "Don't call us that!" She glared at Aladdin again. "Mukhtar could tell we were good workers. He can't run this place on his own. Right, Mukhtar?"

"Right, right," Mukhtar said absentmindedly, and finally looked at Aladdin again. "Again, I'm sorry to have scared you. You fit the description of someone who was meant to work with me a long time ago, and I got confused." His eyes flitted back to the necklace again.

Aladdin closed his hand tightly over the charm. It was warm to the touch, but not burning as it had been before. "So do you still want my necklace?"

"No. Keep your charm. It's . . . better off with you. Family history and all." Still, Mukhtar couldn't stop staring at it. Finally he brightened. "You can get me something better tomorrow when you go out to work with the others. You are staying in Agrabah, no?"

Aladdin had never experienced a day quite like this one. When was the last time he saw a parade, watched a new grand vizier grandstand in front of a city, survived a sandstorm, rescued a monkey, and possibly made friends? Never, that's when. Another whole day in Agrabah made his heart want to soar. But then he remembered. Elham and the others were waiting for him. His heart seemed to weigh down his chest again. "I wish I could, but I have to get back to my tribe. I'm sure they're looking for me."

"One more day," Mukhtar pressed. "Just one. We've barely gotten to know you."

"I can't," Aladdin said sadly. Abu jumped from his shoulder to a table full of trinkets and picked up something shiny and gold. The monkey's eyes widened in awe.

"Don't leave Agrabah," Kalila pressed him. "There's so much to see and do here, and you had less than a day to explore!"

"And the sandstorm messed up part of it!" Malik added.

Aladdin looked ar Mukhtar again, who was staring at the necklace. "I'm on the kids' side. You belong here in Agrabah. Not just because I want you to contribute something. The monkey technically did that for you." He smirked at Fatima. "As if I didn't already see you take those jewels from the monkey!"

Fatima smiled sweetly. "I was about to tell you about them."

"Yeah, yeah," Mukhtar said, ruffling the hair on the top of her head. He seemed more relaxed again, which made Aladdin's stomach uncoil, too. "I've trained them well and I can train you, too," he said to Aladdin. "I think I could teach you a lot actually. You should stay." Aladdin felt that pull in his chest again. The same one he felt when he was staring at that princess in her perfect palace. Something about Agrabah was calling to him. It wasn't just that voice in his head. There was a part of him that knew there was more here than met the eye. "I wish I could, but as soon as this storm lets up, I should go."

Mukhtar nodded. "Loyalty. Good quality. Well, if you change your mind — if you *ever* change your mind." He hesitated. "You know where to find us."

"I think the storm is letting up," Malik said, peeling back a rug covering the window to see outside. "You'll be home in no time."

"I'll walk you to the edge of the city," Kalila said sadly. "I guess Abu will be going with you?"

Abu and Aladdin looked at each other. It was true they'd only met a few hours ago, but they'd been through a lot together. Maybe he was being bananas, but it felt like the monkey was looking out for him when Fatima had picked on him. Aladdin couldn't imagine saying goodbye to the little furry thief. "If he wants to come with me. What do you say, Abu?"

Abu didn't hesitate. He dropped the gold in his paws and jumped onto Aladdin's shoulder again, clinging on for dear life.

Malik opened the door. Dust was still filtering around the air, but the sky was definitely brighter. "It was nice meeting you, Aladdin."

Aladdin didn't want to go yet, but he knew he had to. He'd been gone too long already. Kalila stepped out in front of him. "Yeah, you too. All of you." Mukhtar was still watching him.

"We'll be right here if anything . . . changes," Mukhtar said.

"Time to get you home," Kalila said, reluctantly leading the way.

Aladdin followed Kalila out the door, his feet feeling heavier than they had before. The streets were quiet. Most people were still holed up inside their homes and shelters, but Aladdin could see some returning to life as windows began to open and people peered out doors. A thin layer of dust covered most surfaces, the sand crunching beneath his feet and small particles still drifting through the air. People would be cleaning up for days. Kalila sidestepped a woman sweeping dust out of her doorway while Aladdin narrowly avoided getting doused with a bucket of water someone was tossing onto a dusty window. Abu screeched angrily as the water drenched his back.

"They didn't mean it, Abu," Aladdin told him, and the monkey quieted.

Kalila looked back at him with amusement. "It's like he can understand you."

Aladdin stared at the monkey. "I really think he can." Abu winked. *Did that really just happen?* Aladdin wondered.

They turned another corner, and Aladdin saw the walls of Agrabah fall away. His adventure, if that's what he wanted to call it, was over. He was returning to the Bedouin, and he knew he should be grateful for the day he'd had, but there was a part of him that was sad. If only he could stay with Kalila and the others longer. Really explore the city! But wishing for things didn't make them reality. The edge of the city was near, and beyond it was a world he'd continue to cross. From this vantage point, if he looked to his right, he could still see the dust storm swallowing up land as it crossed the open land. But when he looked left to where his caravan had set up camp, all he saw was . . . sand. His mouth went dry.

"What's wrong?" Kalila asked, seeing his expression.

Aladdin stared at the empty dunes and blinked hard. For a moment, he could almost see the Bedouin encampment in his mind — dozens of tents of varying sizes and animals and people milling about — but then it was gone again. A classic desert mirage. Abu whined quietly, sensing Aladdin's discomfort.

He turned to the girl he'd only known for a short while, trying to quiet the panic rising in his chest. "My tribe," Aladdin said in surprise. "They're gone."

SIX

A laddin stared painfully at the sand in front of him that stretched to the mountains with no sign of a caravan of camels or any people, and focused on his breathing. The Bedouin were gone. But that was impossible. Elham and Sayed Khalid would never have left without him. The tribe didn't leave anyone behind. So where did they go? How would he find them? What did he do if he couldn't? Aladdin tried not to panic.

This is all my fault. I shouldn't have left the marketplace! He pictured Elham calling his name over and over, searching for him before finally having to grab Walid, Yusuf, and Lina and head for shelter. Aladdin looked around for a hill — sometimes they'd ridden out storms on a dune because sandstorms stuck close to the ground. Usually the tribe took to their tents and prayed the wind didn't dismantle them, but the tents weren't here. There were no large boulders in the foreground to crouch behind. Maybe they wet garments to put over their eyes (humans weren't like camels that could shut their nostrils completely and rely on their two sets of long eyelashes to keep the sand out) and ran for safety. But where? *They must be looking for me*, Aladdin decided. He knew he wasn't technically family, but Elham wouldn't have abandoned him. Yusuf and Walid maybe, but not Elham. And yet, she was nowhere to be seen. He was alone.

"My tribe should be here and they're not," Aladdin whispered. Abu whined again, confused. Aladdin looked at Kalila. "Maybe they're seeking shelter somewhere in the city."

Kalila nodded. "I'm sure that's what they're doing. They wouldn't have just left you! You're family."

Aladdin felt his heart start to beat out of his chest. *Family*. Elham had always treated Aladdin like her own, but he'd always felt like an outsider, adrift like a particle of sand moving across the desert. He had been restless. He'd longed for a permanent home instead of a traveling one and now fate had dealt him a hand he wasn't expecting. Agrabah was a big city. What if he couldn't find the Bedouin? Elham would look for him, of course, but after a while, the Bedouin would have to move on without him. Aladdin exhaled slowly. It was one thing to wish for a different life. It was another entirely to suddenly find yourself thrust into a new one without being prepared for it. Aladdin tried to keep his legs from giving out from under him. "This is all my fault."

"What do you mean?" Kalila asked.

Aladdin faced her. "I walked away from the marketplace. I wasn't supposed to, but I wanted to see the city so badly. Then I saw the parade and you swinging from rooftops, and I followed you and lost track of time. I didn't see the signs that a storm was coming till it was too late, and now I'm lost." He blinked rapidly. He would not cry. Even though, if there was ever a time to cry, this was it. *How could I be so reckless? Elham always tells us to stay close at marketplaces so we're not lost for this reason.*

Kalila thought for a moment. "You said you were selling things at the marketplace, right? Maybe they found shelter there. Come on! Let's look!" She grabbed Aladdin's arm and steered him back to the city.

The streets were still pretty empty when they reached the market. Even though Aladdin had been there that morning, the place looked entirely different. Permanent stands were covered with tarps and rugs and still closed, while the tiny makeshift stand he'd stood at with Elham had all but disappeared. There were very few people selling again — just one man trying to sell dates and bread. Aladdin remembered seeing him that morning and rushed over.

"Excuse me," Aladdin said.

"Do you need bread? Dates?" the man blurted out hopefully, holding a loaf in his hand. "I've got them both half price! End-of-day sale!"

"They're covered in sand," Kalila said skeptically.

"Nah! All good! Just brush it off," said the man, who did just that and started to cough. "See? All good."

Aladdin eyed Kalila. "Uh, thanks, but we're actually looking for some vendors that were here this morning. We were standing next to you actually. We had a multicolored cloth on our half of the table? The woman I was with gave you a beaded bracelet for your wife?"

"Ah, yes." He held up his wrist, which now bore the bracelet. "A woman and two boys; they packed up quickly when the storm approached," he said. "Didn't wait it out like I did hoping to get more sales." A breeze blew more sand off his loaf of bread and he sneezed.

"Do you know where they went? Did they shelter somewhere in the city?" Aladdin asked hopefully. "Did you hear them looking for anyone before they left?"

The man shook his head. "No idea. I didn't see them looking for anyone, but again, when the storm came in that fast, everyone just scattered."

Aladdin's heart sank. *Did they forget I was here?* he wondered. "Thank you."

"Are you sure you don't need bread? Seventy-five percent off! Two for one! Any deal you want to make!"

"No thanks," Kalila said as she led Aladdin away from the market area, which was a good thing because his legs suddenly felt like honey.

"Where are we going? I might as well stay here and just work for that guy," he said glumly. "Maybe my tribe will come looking for me, and if they don't, at least I have somewhere to go."

"You already have somewhere to go," Kalila sang. "You heard Mukhtar — he wants you to work with us. You'll come back with me and live in the shop with the rest of us till you find your tribe, or who knows?" She shrugged. "Maybe you'll want to stay in Agrabah. Our place is tight, but it's home."

Home. Aladdin felt a tingling in his neck again. He looked down the street toward the exit from the city and then back at the palace in the distance. There was something about this city that he was drawn to, even though he couldn't put his finger on what it was. That recklessness had cost him, though. What if he never found Elham again? Aladdin's stomach churned. Could he really just stay in Agrabah and work with Kalila and the others? "Are you sure he will take me in?"

"Of course!" Kalila exclaimed. "Abu, too!"

Abu jumped up and down screeching as if this was a great idea.

"And if your tribe comes back, we'll know," Kalila insisted. "No one can keep a secret in this city. We'll hear if someone is looking for you."

"You do spend a lot of time on the streets," Aladdin realized. "Maybe we'll find them when we're working." He looked at her again. "Are you sure about this? You don't even know me."

"I know enough," Kalila said with a smile. "We've got a good thing going with Mukhtar — we are surviving and thriving, and you will, too. I think you'd fit right in. We'll show you the ropes, so come on." She held out her hand. "Do you trust me?"

He stared at her outstretched hand. He'd only known this girl for a few hours, but she'd kept him safe in a sandstorm and helped him navigate the largest city he'd ever seen. If he was going to put his faith in someone, it was Kalila.

Aladdin grabbed her hand. "I trust you." Abu clapped his paws. "Lets go see Mukhtar. Again."

When they arrived a short while later, and Kalila explained what happened, Mukhtar didn't seem very surprised.

"I knew it!" he said, jovial. "Agrabah calls to you. That's why you're still here. Come! Let me properly show you around the charm shop."

"Charm shop?" Aladdin questioned as Abu scurried down his arm and accepted a bowl of water from Malik. Fatima did not look pleased to see him again so Aladdin kept his focus on Mukhtar.

"Yes!" Mukhtar banged a wall with his elbow and a hand-painted canvas sign unrolled from the ceiling that said MUKHTAR'S MAGICK SHOP. "I sell items that are charmed or 'magicked.'"

"What is *magicked*?" Aladdin asked. He'd heard the other kids use the word several times and he hadn't known what it meant.

Mukhtar's gray eyes sparkled as he stood behind a table piled high with silver items that needed a good polish. "They're things that have a touch of magick to them that find their way to me so that I can get them to their rightful owners." He held up a magnifying glass. "See this? If you say the right words three times, and look through it with your right eye on a moonlit night in the summer months, you just might see the future."

Aladdin eyed the item in amazement. "Wow."

"And this?" Mukhtar held up a small velvet bag, much like the one Abu nabbed, and dumped the contents into his hands. It was several gray-and-black rocks. "These are priceless."

"They're rocks," Aladdin noted.

"They're *protector* rocks," Mukhtar said. "Place them around your head when you sleep, and they will ward off evil." He looked at Aladdin curiously. "You definitely need some of these. Here. An early paycheck from me." He put the rocks back in the bag and placed the bag in Aladdin's hands.

Aladdin looked at them in awe. "And they'll work. Really?"

Mukhtar nodded. "You just have to believe, kid. It's like this item here." He held up a tarnished lamp. "Some would say this is just an ordinary lamp meant to hold oil, but me?" He rubbed at the top of the lamp with a cloth. "I say it's magick! There's a genie in here. I can feel it." He rubbed harder and Aladdin watched in wonder, waiting to see a genie unfurl from the lamp in a cloud of smoke. Nothing happened. Mukhtar put the lamp down. "He's in there. He just isn't ready to come out yet. But someday . . . someday I'm going to get wishes from this thing." He held the lamp out to Aladdin. "Want to rub the lamp and meet a genie?"

Abu screeched and jumped on Aladdin's back before settling on his right shoulder. "Are you sure? I don't want to steal your wishes."

"Nah!" said Mukhtar. "You only get three, right? Then you can give the lamp with the genie back to me. Try it!" He handed the lamp over.

Aladdin felt the weight of the lamp in his hands. It was heavy. Were genies heavy? Aladdin wasn't sure. Abu leaned over to get a closer look at it. The lamp needed a serious cleaning, but Aladdin guessed an item didn't have to shine to be beautiful. He tried to twist off the knob on top, but it was wedged tight. *Three wishes*, he thought. *Make three wishes.*

"You have to say the wishes out loud for them to work," Mukhtar added.

"I wish . . . I wish . . ." Aladdin wondered what exactly it was he wanted. He'd never been offered a wish before. He'd never been given a present before. He could wish to find Elham and the others, but would Mukhtar be offended to learn that he was feeling a bit home-sick? Better to think of something else. He knew right away what the wish would be. He closed his eyes. "I wish for a home of my own!" He waited a beat, then opened his eyes. Nothing happened.

Fatima burst out laughing. "I can't believe you fell for that shtick!" Malik laughed, too, holding his stomach.

Kalila took the lamp from Aladdin's hand and thrust it back at Mukhtar. "Stop messing with him."

"I'm not messing with him!" Mukhtar said indignantly. "Magick is real!"

"It's a gimmick for the shop," Fatima argued, giving Aladdin a pointed look. "We 'find' Mukhtar things, and he resells them under the guise they're charmed."

"He says Agrabah is full of magick and it's our job to find the items that need safekeeping," Malik said with an eye roll.

"It's true!" Mukhtar insisted.

This was the second time today that Aladdin heard people talking about enchantments. It was something they never talked about in his caravan. Sayed Khalid hated talk of "such nonsense." But in Agrabah, Aladdin was starting to think, the world worked differently. "So you think magick is real?"

"I know it is," Mukhtar said swiftly.

Aladdin swallowed hard. "Have you ever been to the Night Bazaar, then?"

Mukhtar's eyes widened and the other kids looked at him.

"How do you know about the Night Bazaar?" Kalila whispered.

"It's not real," Fatima insisted. "It's an Agrabah myth!"

"No, it's real," Malik said, jumping up and sitting on one of the long tables. "I've heard people talk about the things they've seen there. The bazaar appears out of nowhere! It's like the marketplace, but not everyone can see it or purchase items from it."

"They say the vendors who work there never leave," Kalila whispered. "They're ancient, but they never age. If that's not magick, I don't know what it is."

"If it's real, I'd love to see it, but you have to be invited, and the bazaar has never shown itself to me," Malik said wistfully.

"Shown itself?" Aladdin questioned.

"Apparently it appears out of nowhere only to those it deems worthy," Kalila explained. "The bazaar protects itself or something like that. And no one else can see the bazaar even though it appears right in the middle of Agrabah."

"Whoa," Aladdin whispered as Abu screeched in agreement. "I heard two men talking about it this morning when I was in the market. One man was mad he couldn't find the doorway to enter."

"It's not like a house — you can't just knock and enter," Mukhtar explained. "If the Night Bazaar feels you're worthy to visit it, it will appear when you need it to."

"Mukhtar has been there before," Kalila told Aladdin. "But he won't talk about it."

"It's too hard to put into words," Mukhtar said, his eyes taking on a dreamy look. "Plus, you talk too much about something special and you might find you don't get invited back. I don't want to offend the place." He stared off at a lantern flickering on a nearby table. "I want to go back. There's still things I need to explore."

"So how do you find it?" Aladdin pushed.

Mukhtar shook his head. "Kid, I told you. If you're meant to see the Night Bazaar, you'll get your chance, but" — he pointed a finger stained with polish at the group — "if any of you get in, you know what to do."

"Bargain for magicked items," Malik, Fatima, and Kalila said together.

"Even though we've never seen any of the junk in this shop possess an ounce of magick?" Malik said under his breath.

"Our items are real!" Mukhtar exclaimed. "When the magick wants to reveal itself, it does. One thing you have to know about magick, Aladdin," he said, moving in close so that his chest was practically bumping Aladdin's, "you can't let it fall into the wrong hands."

"Here we go again," Malik muttered to himself.

"I mean it," Mukhtar growled. "Magick can do a lot of good, and grant you wishes beyond your wildest imagination, but when the wrong people get ahold of it . . ." He shook his head and then stared at Aladdin's necklace so intently, Aladdin started to feel a bit uncomfortable. "It can be extremely dangerous. It's our job to protect the magick in the world. We only sell enchanted items to people who know how to use them properly. Do you understand? We are keepers of magick."

Fatima yawned and muttered to herself. "Such a yarn."

"But what if someone brings home an item that isn't enchanted?" Aladdin had to wonder. He wasn't even sure magick was real! "How can you even tell something has magick properties?"

He glanced at Kalila, who was mouthing, "You can't."

"You'll learn," Mukhtar said, "just like these guys have. We are not thieves — we are keepers of magick, returning items to people who know how to use them properly. There's a difference."

"And if we grab something without magick, the regular stuff sells well, too," Fatima told him, spinning around the room. "Especially bracelets."

"And scarves!" Malik added.

"But magick items go for the most money and are the most important!" Mukhtar insisted. "And that's why my shop is one of the most popular in Agrabah! People searching for magick items know to come to me. Been in business since before you lot were even born and I'll be here . . ." He trailed off, sighing and looking out the shop window, lost in thought. "For a long time. But someday . . . I'm going to convince that genie to pop on out and give me one wish."

"They grant three," Fatima reminded him, suddenly launching herself into a handstand and walking across the room, narrowly missing Malik.

"I just need one," Mukhtar said softly. "I don't want much. There's some things I've done that I wish I hadn't. Some things I feel bad about." He looked at Aladdin. "But I'm going to try to make them right. Never too late for a change, right, there, Al?"

"It's Aladdin," Aladdin corrected him.

Mukhtar shrugged. "I'm calling you Al. And you know what, Al? Someday I'm getting that wish and I'm going on a grand adventure. There's things out there I've got to see through, you know?"

"An adventure," Aladdin repeated. It was kind of what he was on right now, in this shop with these kids and Mukhtar and Abu. It had started off scary — losing Elham and the others, but he suddenly had hope everything would turn out okay. "I like the sound of that."

"Good!" Mukhtar said, pounding his fist on the table. "Who knows? Maybe you'll go with me, kid. But for now? You've got a job with me and a place to stay as long as you like."

Abu made a small noise, reminding Aladdin he was there.

"What about Abu? Can he stay, too?" Aladdin asked.

Mukhtar looked at the monkey, who had seemingly made his eyes go wide and appear innocent. "Yeah, he can stay, too. We've got work to do in this city. There's magick to be found, and we're going to find it and protect it."

"Whatever you say," Fatima said with a yawn.

"Tomorrow you begin, kid," Mukhtar said.

"But I still don't know how to find magick things," Aladdin said, feeling the panic rising in his chest.

"The others will show you all you need to know," Mukhtar promised.

"Mukhtar has a long list of Mukhtarisms that we'll teach you," Malik told Aladdin. "Pretty soon you'll know them all by heart. Well, maybe not all."

"There are currently seventy-seven of them," Kalila revealed.

Aladdin's jaw dropped. "Seventy-seven?"

"Seventy-seven Mukhtarisms! Clever, huh? See, I can come up with good names!" Mukhtar chuckled. "We still need to come up with a new name for you all, though — tribe? Caravan?" The kids shook their heads. "We'll figure it out. But for now, just rest. You've had a big day, Aladdin, and we're so happy you found us." He looked as if he wanted to say more as he stared at Aladdin's necklace again, but instead, he turned toward the door and a stairway beyond it.

Fatima went behind a curtain and came back with several mats. She threw one at Aladdin. "For you to sleep on."

Aladdin wrapped his arms tight around the mat. He'd never slept anywhere but under the stars. Again, he thought of Elham. She'd always said the stars would guide him and in the shop, he couldn't see them. "Where do we sleep?"

"Right here, on the floor," Malik said, tossing Aladdin a pillow.

"It's not much, but it's home for now," Kalila said with a shrug, and handed Aladdin a piece of bread. "But someday we're going to sell enough magicked items to get a place as big as the palace."

"Keep dreaming, Kalila," Fatima said with a yawn.

Aladdin broke off a chunk of bread for Abu, who took it greedily, then took a piece for himself, putting the rest in his pocket for later. They settled down on their mat — their own mat! — and Abu cuddled up on the pillow — Aladdin's own pillow! He was used to the Bedouin, all of whom shared everything.

"I'm in the room above the shop if anyone needs me," said Mukhtar, going to the front door and bolting it shut. Then he turned and headed toward the stairs. "Sleep tight."

Aladdin felt the weight of the day starting to make him sleepy. He laid his head back on the pillow and looked up at the rafters above his head. It was only then he noticed there were several silver stars hanging from strings that glittered in the moonlight. *Look at that*, he thought. *I'm still sleeping under the stars.*

"Rest up, Aladdin," Malik called out as Aladdin heard Fatima start to snore. "Tomorrow your real training begins."

"Should I be nervous?" Aladdin asked, trying to sound anything but.

"Nope!" Kalila told him. "Trust us, Aladdin. We have your back."

SEVEN

MUKHTARISM NUMBER 12:
KEEP YOUR FRIENDS CLOSE.

Despite the comforts of his own mat and pillow, Aladdin's sleep was restless. He dreamed Elham and Lina were wandering around in the middle of a sandstorm, frantically calling for him before the storm overtook them. He'd woken up in a cold sweat just before dawn.

It's just a dream, he told himself, but still he couldn't fall back to sleep. He was used to rising before the sun anyway, so he decided to get up. Today, he'd prove his worth to the group.

By the time the others started to stir, and he heard the creak of the floorboards as Mukhtar began moving around upstairs, Aladdin had already rolled up his mat. Now he was standing at the door with Abu on his shoulder, ready to begin his day.

"Someone's excited to get out there," Malik noted.

"I am," Aladdin admitted, and Abu screeched in agreement. "It's a new day. A new job in a new city. What's not to be excited about?" His life had changed rapidly since he'd arrived in Agrabah just a day ago, and nightmares aside, there had to be a reason he'd found

Kalila and Mukhtar. That tingling sensation on his neck was back.

"Give us a minute," Fatima said. "Not all of us are excited about being up at dawn."

"Fatima is not a good early riser," Kalila whispered with a giggle.

"Her crankiness wears off in a few hours . . . usually," Malik added.

Aladdin didn't mind crankiness. He was just happy to learn how one scouted for an enchanted artifact. Imagine if he found one on his first day on the job?

"Good luck out there today. . . ." Mukhtar paused as he made his way down the stairs. "Crew! What do you think? Is *crew* better than *street rat*? Mukhtar's magicked crew?"

"Maybe," Kalila said. "*Crew* could grow on me."

Mukhtar glanced at Aladdin. "And take care of our newest recruit. Teach him the Mukhtarisms, all right?"

"First Mukhtarism," Kalila started to say. "Number twelve: Keep your friends close."

"Stay close," Aladdin repeated. "Got it!"

Kalila grabbed a large sack from the corner of the room while Malik picked up what looked like a beard. Fatima thrust a sack at Aladdin.

"Hold this for me and keep up. We move fast." She looked him up and down. "Let's see how you do out there. Not everyone can cut it in Agrabah."

Abu screeched indignantly, and Aladdin felt a twinge of annoyance rise within him. Cranky or not, Aladdin didn't like what she was implying. While Kalila and Malik had been welcoming, Fatima definitely seemed irritated by his joining the crew. "Well, I can. Abu and I have got this."

Malik opened the door, letting in a huge swath of bright sunlight. "After you, newbie."

Aladdin stepped out into the alley. Fatima may not have been happy with the early start time, but it seemed the rest of Agrabah was already up. The woman in the stucco home above him was peering out her window while a man down the street slowly pushed a peddler cart full of lamps.

Now that he wasn't running for his life from a dust storm, Aladdin could stop to really appreciate his new city. The street Mukhtar's shop was on was a narrow one with other stucco homes of various sizes — some a few stories high, some smaller like Muckhtar's. Aladdin took a good look at his shop owner's door. He hadn't noticed the details of it when he'd first arrived with Kalila during the storm. The door was an unusual red shade with a hand-carved panel above it that featured a dozen stars painted yellow. None of the other doors on the avenue looked anything like it.

As the group rounded a corner to the next street, Aladdin noticed the sky up above was hazy and a faint blue, as if the sun hadn't agreed to show up yet. The air was still cool, but he knew from experience the day would heat up quickly. Maybe that was why people were already hanging laundry on rope lines that connected one building to the next. Best to get your chores done early, as he knew from his caravan. People were climbing ladders to rooftops or washing clothes and chatting or beating rugs. Down below, he could hear people greeting one another on the street and noticed a guard on patrol.

Kalila stepped in front of Aladdin and stuck out her arm, practically pushing him into an empty alleyway. "Another Mukhtarism," she told him, sounding breathless already at daybreak. "Try not to attract the guards. We stay invisible when we're collecting magick things. That's how we avoid getting caught."

"Invisible," Aladdin said as Abu made a little noise and crawled from one shoulder to the other. "Got it." He paused. "How do we do that?"

Malik tossed him a large piece of fabric. "We like disguises and we use them to stay below the radar." Malik was wearing an identical one in a muted gray like a head scarf, so Aladdin did the same. "Let's start with the basics. How do you create a diversion?"

"Uh . . ." Aladdin looked at Abu, who just gaped.

"I sprained an ankle! I have a headache! I'm lost!" Fatima threw out. "Some sort of injury to draw a crowd and get lost in it, then slip away from them if a shopkeeper or a guard spots you grabbing something magicked and is on your tail."

"Then you go hide, and thankfully there's a lot of great places to hide in Agrabah," Malik told him as they headed into a more populated area. He pulled his hood tighter around his head.

"Where do I hide?" Aladdin said. "Do I go back to the shop?"

"No!" they all said at the same time.

"Never the shop," Malik told him. "I like the tower above the bazaar — which is also a great place to watch the sun rise — or the fish market, which smells so bad the guards usually steer clear."

"How long do you hide?" Aladdin wondered.

"Once I hid for three days," said Malik.

"Wow," said Aladdin. "That's a long time."

Malik shrugged. "A shopkeeper saw me grab a valuable jewel Mukhtar said was magicked, and I had to wait them out till they found another fish to fry."

"I usually grab a roll on my way into hiding in case I'm stuck there for a while," Kalila said as she braided her hair on the go, as if it were the easiest thing in the world. "If you happen to be running past the palace, they offer free meals, too."

"No one likes to hide out on an empty stomach," Fatima warned.

"Hiding spots, royal guards, bread," Aladdin repeated, trying to commit the tips to memory. "What else?"

"The best place to find magicked items obviously is the market," Malik said. "Especially on a weekend."

"Why a weekend?" Aladdin asked as he narrowly missed being run over by two peddler carts being pushed at top speed.

"Most of Agrabah's residents work from sunup to sundown all week long," Fatima explained, shooting the peddlers who were kicking up dust a dirty look. "They have just a few hours one morning each week to do their shopping. Peddler carts begin jockeying for prime positions before dawn, which is why these two are racing to get to the market — they're already late."

"Setting up closest to the palace gates is said to give a seller the best luck," Kalila added. "The worst spot is near the horse corral, which reeks of manure."

"Ugh," Malik said, shivering. "Might be even worse than the fish market, which, as smelly as it is, is still a prime location."

"Standing near Hasim's hokey magic lamp cart is not," Fatima added. "I don't care what Mukhtar says — Hasim's lamps are not magicked."

"But working the street market is," Malik offered as they entered the large open area. Colorful rugs hung on walls that bordered the space where people jockeyed for position around small tables and crudely carved wooden stations with items for sale. A few of the stalls appeared permanent, with colorful green-and-blue wooden doors on them. People also sold items from trunks open on the ground, full of wares. The area was busier than anything Aladdin had seen so far.

"It's crowded, easy to get lost in, and is the perfect place for street performers," Kalila noted as Malik grabbed an empty crate from the peddler cart nearest him and placed it on the ground. He was setting something up.

Aladdin looked around in wonder and couldn't believe his eyes.

Street performers was not the word. There were sword swallowers! Men playing the violin and the flute! An artist drawing the scene around them! As the crowds cheered for someone playing the oud, Fatima and Malik slipped past him.

"Watch and learn," Fatima said. "Be on the lookout for magick!"

"Wait," Aladdin said. "How do I know if something is magicked?"

"You'll know," Kalila said, putting a finger to her lips and following the others.

"How?" Aladdin craned his neck to look back at Abu. "I don't know what they want me to do, Abu! What does a magicked item look like?"

Abu shrugged as if to say *Beats me.*

Yes, his new friends had given him a few Mukhtarisms, but nobody had showed him exactly how to find the items Mukhtar wanted. Aladdin had no clue what a magicked item looked like or how one called to a person. There had to be more to this system. Looking at Fatima or Malik, Aladdin noted all they had was a crate Malik seemed to have "borrowed" to use as a drum. How would that lead them to magick? Aladdin watched the pair anxiously as they began to play. Aladdin expected them to sound terrible, but they were actually decent!

He tucked himself into a corner and stood on a water barrel to watch the pair as they drew a crowd. Malik took off his taqiyah and placed it on the ground for tips.

"I don't get it, Abu," Aladdin whispered, talking to the little monkey as he had once talked to Lina. He was pretty certain the monkey understood him. "They're just performing. How is this a way to find magick items?"

"Those kids are making such a fuss no one is coming to my stand," a shopkeeper lamented.

"Leave them alone," said another man, standing alongside a woman with two babies strapped to her back. "They're just trying to make an honest wage."

Another mother shuffled a few children to the front of the crowd to watch Fatima and Malik's act and then headed off to buy her items at shop stands. Soon other parents did the same. A bunch of children were now clapping and singing along as Fatima and Malik continued to perform. Kalila, however, was nowhere to be found. Aladdin kept his eyes on the others, waiting for something to happen or for magick to appear to him.

"Make way for the Sultan's Royal Guard!" a voice shouted, and Aladdin stood up straighter. A hush fell over the crowd as a group of men moved in two straight lines, their faces stoic, their eyes pingponging from carts to people. They took one look at the crowd gathered in the courtyard and stopped short to watch. Fatima and Malik kept performing, but Aladdin wasn't sure what to do. If the guards were hanging around, there was no way he could grab a magicked item, even if it called to him.

"Free breakfast for our Sultan's Royal Guard at the palace!" a female voice suddenly shouted.

Free breakfast? The guards looked at one another. Aladdin looked at Abu. That voice sounded awfully familiar. No one passed up free breakfast, but something told him to stay put even if his stomach was starting to growl.

"Men, let's go!" the first guard declared, and they began moving again in two straight lines toward that sweet voice and whatever food awaited them.

The rest of the crowd turned back to their shopping and their entertainment, watching Fatima and Malik again. But before Aladdin could walk over to ask them if he should be looking for anything magicked, the crowd began to part. An old beggar woman, her head covered in a piece of teal fabric, was slowly making her way down the first row of carts, walking so slowly that even grandmothers shook their heads and hurried around her and her cane, which she stopped to adjust every few seconds.

Her cane banged into Aladdin.

"Sorry, dearie," she croaked in a voice that sounded as tough as leather. "Move around! Move around! Don't mind me. I have all day and only one thing to buy." She bumped into a young mother and baby watching Fatima and Malik. "So sorry, dearie! What a love," the woman croaked, raising her hand to touch the child.

"Thank you," the young mother said. "We should be — Oh!" She backed into Malik, who came out of nowhere behind her. The woman's market purchases, fresh fruit and bread, fell to the ground, the apples rolling down the street.

"I've got them!" said Malik. He gathered up the fruit and bread and placed it back in the woman's bag. "Here you go, ma'am. I'm so sorry about that, but the fruit looks fine. Really juicy! Should be no harm done."

"Thank you! What a nice young man," the woman said, reaching into her bag again and bringing out a shiny red apple. "Here. For your help."

"Oh, ma'am, I couldn't take what I haven't paid for," he said solemnly, his hand to his chest.

Aladdin tried not to smirk.

"I insist," said the mother, pressing the apple into his hands as her baby started to wail. "Please."

Malik bowed. "Thank you so much! Have a great day! OH!" He banged into a man clapping along to Fatima's music. "Sorry." He put a hand on the man's shoulder. "Are you okay?"

"Fine. Just fine," said the man.

"Sure thing," said Malik, stopping for a second to watch Fatima.

And slip something shiny in his pocket.

"Magicked," Malik mouthed to Aladdin.

"Ah, Abu." Aladdin watched Malik in amazement. "I think I'm starting to understand how things work. Now I just have to find something magicked that needs saving."

And that's when he heard it — the voice was back.

EIGHT

Aladdin . . . keep your eyes open. . . .

Aladdin shook his head. Why was he hearing things?

Aladdin . . .

No one seemed to react to the voice but him. Aladdin could sense a change in the air the moment he heard it. The crowd had grown unusually quiet. People were still watching Fatima and Malik or shopping, but it was as if Aladdin's world had stopped. Even Abu started whimpering, staring at his new friend curiously. Did he hear it, too? Was this what the others meant about hearing a magicked item call to them?

Look harder. . . .

"Look harder at what?" Aladdin said to no one in particular. A mother glanced at him strangely. Aladdin attempted a meek smile.

And that's when the crowd parted. A man in fine, long velvet robes walked purposefully through the market. He had on more jewels than the Sultan, and his taqiyah was equally adorned. Aladdin noticed the man didn't crack a smile or make eye contact with anyone, but he was clearly taking in the scene with interest as his two bodyguards ushered him through the market. Aladdin could only assume he was headed to the palace to meet with the Sultan.

"Who is that?" someone asked.

"He works for the new grand vizier."

"He doesn't look familiar. Is he from Agrabah?"

"No," said the first. "They say he's traveled from afar with the new grand vizier to help Agrabah."

Why would the voice call to Aladdin to observe this man? Did he have something magicked on him? Maybe!

Curious, Aladdin inched closer, his eyes on the grand vizier's aide's velvet coat. If he could just snag one magicked bracelet from the man's arm, Mukhtar would be pleased. Those jewels were bigger than his fist! Okay, maybe not his fist, but as big as his thumb. He couldn't believe someone who worked for the grand vizier could have such fine things.

Aladdin...

There was the voice again. Was the voice a sign that the grand vizier's aide's jewels were magicked? Aladdin's eyes locked on what the man was holding — a small blue glass vial. It didn't look valuable, but maybe the jar was magicked! Aladdin had a feeling he was right. He reached closer.

One of the bodyguards stepped in front of Aladdin. "Maintain your distance, boy." The guard was bumped from behind.

"Sorry, dearie!" the old woman croaked as she crashed into the bodyguard and sent him stumbling backward into the grand vizier's aide, who fell into a banana cart. Bananas went flying in the air, one pelting the grand vizier's aide in the head.

Aladdin looked up at the old woman in wonder and noticed something familiar about her eyes — it was Kalila.

She winked at him. "You okay, dearie?"

"Fine," said Aladdin, trying not to smirk. "Sorry about that."

"No worries," she said, pushing her cart off again. Meanwhile the grand vizier's aide was still struggling to get up. Aladdin quickly looked at the man's hands. The vial was gone. His eyes scanned the ground. The bottle was rolling away.

Aladdin...

There was the voice again! The bottle had to have magick in it! He needed to move quickly! Aladdin placed Abu on a water barrel, then made his move.

"My fruit!" said the peddler to the aide. "You've ruined my bananas!"

In the commotion, Aladdin's other hand closed around the vial.

"Boy, we need you to step back," said the bodyguard again.

Aladdin clung tight to the vial as he stepped away, backing up and handing it to Abu. "Sorry about that!" he said. Thankfully the monkey seemed to know exactly what Aladdin was doing. When Aladdin turned to look at Abu again, the vial was gone.

"Where is my package?" the panic-stricken aide said, dusting off his robe and staring at Aladdin suspiciously. "Have you seen a small blue bottle?"

"Bottle?" Aladdin repeated with a cock of his head as the beggar woman watched him. "What bottle?" He bent down and pretended to search for it. "What did it look like?"

"Guards? Keep searching!" said the aide. "I could have sworn I had it in my hand, but maybe I left it back at that lamp cart we passed earlier."

The trio went on their way, the grand vizier's aide not even giving Aladdin a second glance. If he had, he would have seen the small smile begin to play on Aladdin's lips.

Aladdin had scored his first magicked item! He couldn't wait to show the others!

And so it went all morning, Fatima and Malik, the old beggar woman, and the dark-haired boy with the great smile, moving through crowds, never acknowledging one another or standing near one another for more than a moment. To the common passerby, they were four strangers. No one noticed the boy with his drumming crate slowly filling up the box with magicked trinkets or the beggar woman's satchel thickening. No one realized the boy with the big smile and the cute monkey who performed tricks for eager children were scouting magicked items.

Aladdin hadn't heard the voice again, but he could feel the vial Abu had given back to him burning a hole in his baggy trousers. He was curious about it, but knew it wasn't safe to examine the bottle in the open. Was it truly magicked? What made it magicked? And why was the grand vizier's aide so upset about losing it? The bodyguards thankfully hadn't come back to search the area again at least. Whatever was inside that bottle couldn't have been that important for the aide to give up so easily.

The group kept up their ruse for hours. A bracelet was handed off here, a small glass bowl made its way into the beggar cart. The items kept piling up. Aladdin helped where he could, bumping people, distracting others, or showing off Abu till his friends could get away. He didn't sense any of the items calling to him the way the bottle did, but he was new at all this so it wasn't surprising. He was finally starting to get the hang of things when the sun began to lower in the sky and the crowds in the market thinned.

That's when the crew heard a drum sound, saw how the sun was setting, and knew their day was done. They packed up their things and began to depart, one by one, in different directions, never making eye contact with the shopkeepers or the people they had seen earlier in the day. They moved quickly, but not too quickly. Smiled, but didn't smile too much, slipping through the streets, passing the entrance to the Sultan's palace and Agrabah's finest homes till they came to their street.

"Another lamp score!" whispered Kalila. "Mukhtar will be thrilled when he sees this," she said, pointing to the lamp on top of the cart she'd pilfered somewhere along their morning route.

"No wonder you're his favorite!" drawled Fatima, springing forward and doing a front flip. She righted herself and turned to the rest of them. "And what about you, newbie? Sense any magick, Aladdin?"

Aladdin hesitated. Did he tell them about the bottle and how he heard the voice? He glanced at Abu on his shoulder and the monkey just blinked at him. Aladdin kept quiet, soon spotting the familiar red door with the stars above it. The group slipped inside without a sound and found Mukhtar asleep on a chair, snoring loudly.

"Looks like business was lively today," Fatima said wryly. She dropped her things on the floor with a clang and Mukhtar snorted, springing up fast.

"I don't know where it is! I swear!" he shouted, his arms shooting out in front of him. He saw Aladdin and blinked twice, shaking the sleep out of his head. "Oh, it's you. Is it night already?"

"Good nap, Mukhtar?" Malik asked, accidentally upending a rusty tray with oil bottles on it. Kalila rescued it before it crashed to the floor.

"I made a few deals while you were gone," Mukhtar said defensively. "And what about you?" He glanced at Aladdin. "Did you find anything?"

Like the day before, the kids started to go through their magicked finds. There was an unusual golden feather Fatima had plucked from someone's kufi when no one was looking, and a rock that looked like it might be a jewel that Abu grabbed from the banana cart. Both Kalila and Fatima had scored a few small magicked bowls and Malik had even gotten his hand on a sandal.

"A magicked sandal?" Mukhtar sounded doubtful.

Malik shrugged. "It spoke to me. Maybe tomorrow I'll get the other one for you."

Mukhtar chuckled. "Good haul, not that I see anything here that shouts magick to me."

Fatima groaned. "We're always telling you — nothing shouts magick to us, either, but these things *felt* magical. Either way, these goods should bring in money."

"Yes, they should," Mukhtar agreed, and turned to Aladdin. "And what about you, kid? Find anything magicked on your own today?"

Aladdin hesitated for a moment — the others had grabbed jewelry and priceless artifacts. All he had was a small bottle. Could it be magicked?

"Al?" Mukhtar tried again.

Aladdin looked around at the others. Abu shrieked encouragingly and jumped on his right shoulder for what felt like support. Aladdin took a deep breath. "I think I found something magicked." He reached into his pocket and pulled out the small blue bottle.

Everyone leaned over to stare at the item in Aladdin's hands and burst out laughing.

"A magick bottle?" Fatima said.

"That's no magick potion," Malik agreed. "It looks like oil."

"Aladdin," Kalila groaned. "When I saw you with that grand vizier's aide, I thought you were grabbing something good."

Aladdin looked at Mukhtar, who was the only one not laughing. "You don't understand — I felt like the bottle was calling to me. I heard a voice when the bottle was near. As soon as I saw the grand vizier's aide, the marketplace became quiet and I could hear the vial calling out to me. I thought it was enchanted. Isn't that what happens for all of you?"

"Nope," said Malik. "Nothing I grab talks to me."

The others laughed.

"Quiet!" Mukhtar barked, and everyone stopped. Mukhtar took the vial from Aladdin, rolling it in his hands before muttering something no one could hear and popping the top off. The bottle hissed like a snake. Mukhtar turned the bottle over and banged it on his palm. A small scrap of paper fell out.

Malik sidled up next to Mukhtar to read the message. "It says the other half of the charm is within the city walls and may be in possession of something called a diamond. What does that mean? There are diamonds in the market?" he said hopefully.

"Did I tell you you could look at this?" Mukhtar snapped. He turned back to Aladdin. "Where did you find this?"

"I told you—I saw the grand vizier's aide with it in the marketplace." Aladdin didn't understand what he had done wrong.

"And it called to you? You heard a voice?" Mukhtar asked, practically standing nose to nose with Aladdin.

Aladdin blinked. Maybe saying he'd heard a voice was the wrong thing to say. He stared at Mukhtar's expression, though he wasn't sure lying was the better option. "Yes," he said softly. "It was calling my name."

"That's ridiculous," Fatima said with a snort.

"*Fatima,*" Kalila warned.

"Tell me exactly what happened," Mukhtar said quietly.

Aladdin thought hard, trying to remember every detail. "I saw the aide approach and that's when I heard the voice. I only knew he worked for the grand vizier, but the bottle felt important. I wasn't sure why." He found himself getting flustered at the others, snickering.

Mukhtar put a reassuring hand on his shoulder. "Take your time. Tell me about the voice. How did you steal this vial from the aide?"

"Mukhtar, you don't really buy into this voice business, do you?" Fatima asked.

"I've never heard a voice when I found something magicked," Malik seconded.

Aladdin focused on Mukhtar. "I bumped into him — that part was by accident — and he dropped the vial. I grabbed it with my free hand and passed it to Abu before anyone saw."

"Did he realize the bottle was gone?" Mukhtar asked.

"Yes," Aladdin said. "His bodyguards searched for it for a while, but they found nothing. We didn't see them again for the rest of the day."

"No one came back to look for you?" Mukhtar sounded serious. "You didn't let anyone see you with the bottle till you got back here?"

Aladdin shook his head. "No. I gave it to Abu for safekeeping and didn't take it back till later in the day. Why?"

Mukhtar clasped Aladdin's shoulder. "You did good."

"He did?" Fatima asked in surprise. "That bottle isn't magicked! All it had inside was a note that didn't make sense!"

Mukhtar held up the bottle, observing its reflection in one of the lamps lit in the shop. "Don't be deceived by its appearance, Fatima. This bottle is full of magick. *Dangerous* magic. Magic we can't mess with."

"The kind you've warned us about?" Kalila shifted from one foot to the other anxiously.

"Yes." Mukhtar sounded grave. "Tomorrow, we all stay here. Till the bodyguards can no longer remember your faces and lose all interest in finding that bottle."

Fatima moaned. "But the weekends always have the best magicked items!"

"No arguing about this," Mukhtar insisted. "You stay here and stay hidden. In fact, you sleep in my quarters tonight. I'll stay down here."

Abu whined softly. Aladdin's stomach tightened. He had to agree with Fatima on this one. Why was Mukhtar so worried about a scrap of parchment in a tiny blue bottle and a note no one understood? "Mukhtar, what does that message mean?"

Mukhtar ruffled the top of Aladdin's head, then placed the bottle in his pocket for safekeeping. "Nothing for you to worry about. It's going to be my job to make sure they don't find what the note is telling them to look for."

"And what is that?" Aladdin pressed.

Mukhtar just pointed to the stairs. "Up you go. Get some rest."

The four of them filed up the stairs with their blankets, Fatima and Malik still groaning.

"Last night I dreamed I'd find a huge bag of jewels this weekend and we'd have enough money to finally buy a bigger place with three stories," Kalila said wistfully.

"Looks like our palace will have to wait a few more weekends," Malik teased. "What would you buy if we had all the magicked items in Agrabah, Al?"

Aladdin didn't have to think, even for a moment. "Answers."

He wasn't sure why, but something told him Mukhtar was worried for a good reason.

They all grew silent, listening to the muffled sound of Mukhtar moving around below.

What did that note mean by a diamond? Aladdin couldn't help but wonder. *And why is Mukhtar so afraid to share the truth?*

NINE

NASIR

"And then there is the Festival of the Olive Tree, which is my favorite one of the year so we should start planning,"

"Yes, Your Majesty," said Nasir, his voice barely more than a whisper.

"And we always have a dinner party every new moon! And oh! Wait till you see what we do in Agrabah for holidays!" the Sultan continued, clearly excited to have someone back at the helm with him.

Nasir was so bored. He hated having to listen to the Sultan go on and on and on about trivial things, but from what he knew about the Sultan, the guy couldn't make a decision on his own. He surrounded himself with advisers that he trusted implicitly. When his grand vizier had gone to a meeting in his place, Nasir had momentarily felt bad. The storm he'd conjured was meant for the Sultan. Not his grand vizier. Still, making the old grand vizier disappear was as easy as swatting a gnat. Lightning strikes were easy to conjure. What wasn't easy was finding a way to get rid of this nit-witted sultan.

Nasir had thought his plan was foolproof—prove Agrabah's

sultan was inefficient and have him ousted so Nasir could move around the city searching for the artifact without being questioned. Being temporarily in charge meant people would have to bow to his every whim. There would be no questioning his decisions! No complaints that he was being hardheaded *or* hotheaded! People would have to do what he asked of them. But once he found the artifact, his brother could have Agrabah. By birthright, his brother was the one who was meant to rule, and that was fine as far as Nasir was concerned. Let his brother be a sultan. Nasir had bigger plans. He wanted power that extended beyond one small city.

The visons he'd been having told him the other half of the charm was within this city's walls. Once he found it, he could complete the quest set forth for him by the Azalam and they could finally open the Cave of Wonders. No matter how reckless he might be, even he wasn't witless enough to abandon the assignment they'd given him.

Nasir sighed and stared at his reflection in a nearby mirror. He always enjoyed his own reflection. His skin was smooth and taut from all the tonics he used nightly, and his hands were baby soft. He bathed often, using oils and lotions that not only kept him smelling better than any man he knew, but made his skin practically glow. *I am good-looking, aren't I? Much better looking than my older brother . . .*

"And I love to have parties at least once a month so that all our people can gather together as one," the Sultan babbled on, still talking about soirees and gardens and a rehabilitation program he'd been wanting to create for older gazelles. This man was too into animals and being good to his people as far as he was concerned. "Should we have one this week?"

Nasir tore himself away from his reflection. The guy was asking him a question now. "Of course, Your Majesty," he said on autopilot, bowing again. "I will look into it at once."

He wouldn't.

"Oh, Nasir, how lucky I am you stumbled upon Agrabah on your journey," said the Sultan happily. "I think we're going to do wonderful work together."

Wars weren't won by gazelle rescuers. Cities didn't become revered by looking weak or hobnobbing with one's people. The Sultan was doomed.

"Me too, Exalted One," Nasir said, laying it on thick. He touched the gold charm that he wore around his neck absentmindedly. The half beetle was polished to perfection and gleamed bright like the sun. Nasir wore the unusual charm around his neck so that it was never out of his sight. He hadn't taken it off since he "acquired" it so long ago. He just needed the other half and then he could fulfill his destiny . . . er, fulfill the Azalam's orders.

"We will do magnificent things the likes of which Agrabah has never seen," Nasir added for effect. The Sultan's eyes widened in excitement. Too bad those magnificent things Nasir was talking about would have nothing to do with the Sultan.

Soon, the glory would be all his! Nasir had dreamed about this moment for twelve years now, ever since his family had secured half of the charm necessary to open the Cave of Wonders. Sure, it had taken him much longer than he had anticipated to track down the other half, but after a few failed summoning spells, he had a premonition that told him he'd find what he sought in Agrabah. (If he needed more proof, the charm around his neck had warmed to the touch the moment he entered the city.) Now Nasir was one step closer to completing his older brother's mission on behalf of the Azalam: locate the missing half of the charm, gain access to the Cave of Wonders, and then send for his brother so he could receive infinite power. Never mind that they were technically supposed to hand the reunited pieces of the amulet over to higher-ups in the Azalam so they could open the cave. Neither brother planned on doing *that*. No, this glory was meant for them and them alone. The Cave of Wonders that the vizier's father, and his grandfather, and his grandfather's grandfather had long ago prophesied would finally be open and the glory would be all his!

"Ahem."

Nasir turned from his spot in front of the Sultan's throne and saw his faithful servant, Faaris, standing in the shadows. And a few feet behind him was that darn cat the princess favored, looking like he was ready to pounce at any moment. How that mangy beast hadn't eaten someone yet was beyond him. Nasir didn't trust the thing. He beckoned Faaris closer. The man walked in between large stone columns and stood beside a potted plant.

"Your Majesty, I beg your pardon, but my aide has, uh, brought news about the new-moon dinner party you wanted to host." Nasir made a motion to Faaris, who looked utterly confused. Why couldn't the man follow his lead?

"Splendid. I want the whole city invited to this dinner party. My daughter, Jasmine, should be pleased about that." He sighed. "I hope."

"Excellent, Your Majesty," said Nasir, with another annoying bow. "We want our princess to be happy. Will you excuse me for a moment so I can see what, er, plans he has already made to secure the new-moon . . . dinner?"

He walked light-footed and sure to one side of the large chamber as the Sultan watched. Then, with a slight turn of his wrist that would be imperceptible to the nearby guards, Nasir created a clear sound barrier around him and Faaris so that they couldn't be heard.

"Well?" His voice sharpened like a knife. "What have you found?"

Faaris gulped hard, his Adam's apple bobbing up and down. His brow was beaded with sweat, but whose wasn't in this oppressive heat? "Sir, I did as you asked. I got proof that the charm is near, but I didn't understand what the note meant. It said it may be in possession of a diamond."

"A diamond?" Nasir scoffed. "You must have read the message wrong — the charm *is* the diamond! It's the other half of the jewel we've long searched for. Where is the note? I'll read it myself."

Faaris swallowed again. "That's just it . . . I . . ."

"Just spit it out already, Faaris!" Nasir snapped. "I hate when you stammer. And use some tonic. Your face is looking very shiny."

"It's just . . . the note . . . well . . ." Faaris's voice wafted away as he closed his eyes for a moment. "The Azalam placed the information in a small bottle so we wouldn't be seen talking. . . . I think they were fearful the Cave could catch wind and curse them."

"So? Hand me the bottle!" Why was Faaris so incompetent?

"That's just it. They handed the note off to me, and I was hurrying through the marketplace when I . . . lost it."

A flash of heat pulsed through Nasir that he couldn't stamp down. He tried to remain calm so he could continue to hold the sound barrier and not lose it. He was not a patient man. "You lost it? Then find it!"

"I looked everywhere, sir," Faaris said, backing away slightly.

From the darkness, Nasir heard the large cat start to growl. *If that beast stepped any closer . . .* "Looking isn't good enough. Find it!"

Faaris's brown eyes showed his fear. "I want to, but when we returned to the location where I believe I might have dropped it, the bottle was nowhere to be found. I even tried the summoning spell you taught me, but it was as if the vial disappeared. I can't seem to locate it anywhere."

Nasir closed his eyes and tried to exhale slowly. *Of course.*

The Azalam, the group his family had long been a part of, had warned that the closer they got to tracking down the other half of the charm, the tougher their quest would be. His spells had found the charm, but locating it among the people was going to be tougher. And what about this diamond Faaris was blabbing about? Was the other half of the charm made of diamonds? That didn't make sense. He stroked his beard, but it was something to keep in mind. There was something he was missing here. And for that, he might need some magick to help him figure things out. Perhaps a new potion to summon the charm within the city limits. His sorcery skills were far superior to Faaris's. It wouldn't be hard to do, but first he needed ingredients. Where would he find some on such short notice? Hmm . . . he did know of a place that might carry them, but gaining access to it would require some trickery on his part. "I will take care of this myself. But if you fail me again, Faaris . . ."

Faaris breathed what appeared to be a sigh of relief. "I won't, sir."

"You'd better not . . ." Nasir said, a smile easing onto his face (although it was a creepy one that caused way too many wrinkles; he wouldn't hold it for long). Even if Faaris had messed up, Nasir still had confirmation that the charm was closer than it ever had been before. Now he just had to find it.

But first he'd take a luxurious bath to calm his nerves for the second time today. All would be right with the world. "Go. See if you can find anyone in Agrabah who dabbles in the dark arts or magick of any kind. I will need some supplies to do my summoning spell. I think I know how to find some, but if I'm wrong, I need another plan." Faaris moved to leave, but Nasir grabbed his arm. "Don't disappoint me again."

"I won't, sir," Faaris reiterated, disappearing into the shadows in the opposite direction from the large cat.

Nasir took a deep breath. He lowered the sound shield and stepped back into the sunlit room where the Sultan was sitting. The Sultan looked up in surprise, as if he'd forgotten Nasir was even still here. "I have great news, Your Majesty." He thought again of the charm. It was definitely here! In Agrabah! He was so close now! "The dinner plans are proceeding according to plan."

"Excellent!" the Sultan said. "Rejoice, Nasir! This is a glorious day for our people!"

"A glorious day indeed," Nasir said, smiling wide.

And as far as Nasir was concerned, it was only going to get better from here.

After all, who was going to stop him?

TEN

MUKHTARISM NUMBER 5:
DIVERSION TACTICS ARE KEY!
("I SPRAINED AN ANKLE!" OR "I AM LOST!")

For two days, Mukhtar wouldn't let the kids out of his sight. He made up excuses to keep them in the shop longer than originally planned. First, Mukhtar said they needed to take "inventory" of the shop's items — a painstaking task that meant the group had to clean and move every item in the shop including a large magicked oud. (Aladdin couldn't believe the instrument had been smuggled out of the marketplace, but Malik and Fatima both swore they'd been the ones to nab it.) Mukhtar said it had magick in it, but when Abu plucked the strings, it sounded like a regular ol' oud. And Fatima's cymbals sounded like cymbals, and Malik's favorite drum sounded like a drum. The qanun that Abu tried to play sounded so off-key, Mukhtar confiscated the string instrument.

"Abu! Can't you lot do your cleaning in silence?" Mukhtar growled before taking the instrument back upstairs with him.

"I don't think I've ever seen him in such a foul mood," Malik whispered once Mukhtar was out of earshot.

The monkey jumped back onto Aladdin's back and clung to his neck.

"Well, there was that one time Fatima lost that magicked crown Mukhtar wanted to sell," Kalila reminded them.

"Hey!" Fatima did a cartwheel across the floor, then spun around — that girl could never stand still. "I didn't lose it, I just gave it back to the princess. It belonged to her."

"You didn't know for sure it was hers," Malik said. "What would the princess be doing outside the palace without guards?"

"I'm telling you, it was her! Maybe she just needed an escape. We all do sometimes," Fatima insisted, spinning around and around.

Malik groaned. "For the last time, that girl you saw in the head wrap was not the princess of Agrabah!" Malik gestured so wildly, his hands sent a gold urn toppling off the table. Abu caught it before it hit the floor. "Better yet: Why would a princess want to shop in our marketplace? She can have anything her heart desires brought to her."

Kalila took the urn back from Abu and placed it on a high shelf along with the other urns and vases that had already been polished. "Maybe she actually wanted to see the people her father is supposed to serve."

Malik burst out laughing. "Yeah, right! Forget I mentioned the princess. My point is: Mukhtar hasn't been this cranky in a while. What is up with him?"

"Ask Aladdin," said Fatima. "He's the one who set him off."

"Me?" Aladdin stopped wiping a tarnished bracelet and looked at her. "What did I do?"

"You grabbed that ridiculous oil bottle with the cryptic message," Fatima said. "He hasn't been the same since."

"She might be right," Kalila said with a frown, slipping off the bracelets she'd been wearing to polish into the waiting tray. "He's been upset since he read that message that didn't make sense."

"What did it say again?" asked Malik, almost knocking over the oud. Kalila righted it.

"One of the diamonds is near," Aladdin repeated. Suddenly he felt a burning sensation. He looked down and blinked hard. Was his beetle charm glowing? He lifted it off his chest and stared at it, but it looked like it always did — dirty, tarnished, and worth nothing. He was seeing things.

"The diamond . . ." Malik repeated, thinking to himself. "We've never found a jewel that priceless before. I'd remember. They're pretty rare."

"And no one in Agrabah — not even our princess — seems to flaunt one," Fatima said.

They heard the familiar sound of Mukhtar coming down the creaky stairs again, and everyone stopped talking and started polishing again.

"Looks good in here," Mukhtar said. "I don't think I've ever seen the shop this sparkling."

"It will look great when no one comes by to see it," Malik said, and Fatima giggled.

Mukhtar glared at him. "Actually, someone is coming this afternoon and you all can't be here when they do."

"We're being sprung? Thank the stars!" Kalila said gleefully.

Fatima crossed her arms. "Why can't we be here? Who's coming?"

"A buyer," Mukhtar said, "who wants no interruptions from children or primates."

Abu squawked indignantly.

Mukhtar shook his head. "I swear that thing understands me."

"He does," Aladdin insisted. "And he doesn't like being referred to as a primate. Right, Abu?" The monkey nuzzled closer to Aladdin's neck.

"In any case, I'm sending you all out to work," Mukhtar told them. The group cheered. "But today instead of just finding magicked stuff that will help us buy a bigger place, I also have something I need you to get to someone." He unlocked a cabinet Aladdin hadn't noticed before and pulled out a small gold statue. Aladdin heard the other kids audibly inhale. Abu made a tiny squeak and hopped on Aladdin's head, his front paws covering Aladdin's eyes.

"Abu, I can't see!" Aladdin removed the monkey and placed him on the table, where he scampered over to see the small statue. The other kids gathered around, too.

The totem was so small it could fit in the palm of Aladdin's hands. And even though the room was dark, the totem shone bright, showing off its unique shape. It appeared to be two griffins standing back-to-back with one shared set of hind legs. The statue's wings were as long as the creature's body and the griffins' mouths were on a tiny hinge. Right now it was wide-open as if in mid-roar. Aladdin watched as Mukhtar reached into his pocket and pulled out a familiar velvet bag and dumped the contents into his hand.

They were the jewels Abu had stolen. Mukhtar poured the two jewels into one griffin's mouth, then pulled a small scrap of paper out of his other pocket, folded it, and put it inside the totem's other mouth before closing it firmly. He looked up and stared directly at Aladdin. "I need you to get this to Arif at the fish market."

"Aladdin?" Fatima balked at the same time Malik said, "He's a newbie! That should be my job!"

The group's questions were rapid-fire. Abu's head swiveled trying to keep up.

"I thought that griffin was your prized possession in the shop," Kalila chimed in. "You said you'd never trade it!"

"You're hiding something." Fatima narrowed her eyes. "You never make us do jobs without telling us why we're doing them. What's going on?"

"Is this about that bottle that talked to Aladdin the other day?" Malik asked.

"Again, it didn't talk to me, it called to me," Aladdin said.

Malik shrugged. "Same thing."

"It's not," Aladdin insisted, and Abu screeched in agreement. Maybe it was silly to think that Aladdin had found something magicked his first day out.

Mukhtar cleared his throat. "That's enough out of all of you. Since when do you question my decisions? Show some manners!"

"Manners, yeah right," Malik started to joke, and Fatima shot him a look.

"Yes, manners!" Mukhtar's voice boomed, rattling a mirror that had started to desilver, black edges seeping into the glass. "I'm the one who has to keep this place running, aren't I? I'm the one who has to pay the tax collectors, not you. Are you telling me I have to explain why I'm choosing Aladdin to deliver this magicked item?"

"No," they all mumbled.

Mukhtar rolled his shoulders back. "All right, then. It's settled. Aladdin is the right person for this trade and you all will accompany him to deliver it. Understood?" The others nodded.

Aladdin stood up straighter. It was only his fourth day in Mukhtar's Magick Shop and already he was being trusted to do something as valuable as making a trade. He couldn't believe it. "I will make sure this gets to Arif," Aladdin promised.

"I know you will." Mukhtar took Aladdin's left hand and tucked the statue in his palm. "This is yours to guard. See to it that it gets to Arif and *only* Arif. Tell him to open the griffins' mouths before you leave and make sure he gives you something in return. Tell him this gift comes with a price. Understood?" Aladdin nodded. "If he's not working, then you say nothing to the others at the fish market. Just find out when Arif will be back. Got it?"

Aladdin closed his fist firmly around the griffins. "Only give it to Arif, make sure he gives me something in return, and if Arif isn't there, don't hand it over to anyone else. Got it?"

Mukhtar clapped a hand on his shoulder. "You're going to be all right, Al. Just do as I tell you and trust your gut." He hesitated. "I know you can handle this." He pointed a finger at the others again. "And the rest of you — watch out for him. See any funny business or anyone watching you all strangely, distract them and get out of the market immediately."

Aladdin tried not to feel unnerved, even as Abu whined quietly on his back. "Should I be worried?"

"No, no," Mukhtar insisted. "You should always watch your back. And front."

"Mukhtarism number eight," Malik, Fatima, and Kalila echoed.

Mukhtar looked at the others. "Everyone clear on what they have to do?"

"Yes," Fatima, Malik, and Kalila said at the same time.

"Good. Be back by sundown. Understood?"

"Yes," they all repeated, sounding wearier than they had the first time.

Everyone got to work grabbing disguises, instruments, and bags to cart their loot home in. But Aladdin's job was different. He placed the priceless item in his thawb's pocket and waited for the others to finish getting ready.

"Listen, I don't want to scare you, kid, but this job I'm giving you," Mukhtar said, "it's not a typical job."

Aladdin swallowed hard. *Thanks for scaring me*, he thought, but he'd never say it out loud. "Oh?"

Mukhtar nodded. "You may see things you don't understand." He hesitated. "But I know you can handle it. Just keep your head. Think with that! Not your heart! It's an important Mukhtarism."

"I'll remember," Aladdin promised. Mukhtar was giving him his first big assignment, and he would deliver — literally and figuratively. "Besides, I have Abu to protect me, right, Abu?"

The small monkey hopped up and down on Aladdin's shoulder, and he laughed.

Mukhtar, however, still looked pensive. "Stick together. Don't be swayed by things that seem too good to be true. Do what you've been sent to do — don't get caught up in the magick."

"Magick?" Aladdin paused. Mukhtar hadn't said anything about magick being part of this delivery.

Mukhtar clasped Aladdin's hand. "I wish I could go with you, but we can't both go at the same time."

To the market? Suddenly a new thought occurred to Aladdin. His fingers started to tingle. "Wait a minute . . . am I going to the Night Bazaar?"

"Shhh!" Mukhtar pulled him deeper into the corner as the others chattered on nearby. "They know of Arif at the fish market, but he really resides in places that can't be seen by the naked eye. As I told you — people who work at the Night Bazaar can't leave the Night Bazaar." He glanced over his shoulder. "The others don't know where you're actually headed *if* you're deemed worthy." He jutted out his chin. "But I have faith you will be. Don't get distracted. You can only stay for so long . . . unless you get caught up in something you shouldn't be doing."

It's a test, Aladdin thought, feeling his knees quake. *A test to prove I belong here.* He stood up straighter. He was getting a chance to see the Night Bazaar! "I promise. I'll be careful and I'll be back before you know it."

"Keep this between us, Al, and good luck, street . . ." Mukhtar stopped himself again. "How about *team* instead of *crew*? Good luck, team?"

"Ehh," the kids said.

Aladdin gave a small wave and followed the others out the door. For such an exciting task, he wished Mukhtar didn't look so dour. All Aladdin had to do was get into the Night Bazaar, deliver the totem, and get out. Everything would be fine.

He hoped.

ELEVEN

MUKHTARISM NUMBER 19:
NEVER HIDE WHERE YOU SLEEP.

As soon as Aladdin stepped outside, Fatima tried to reach into his thawb pocket, where the totem was resting safely.

"Hey!" Aladdin was quicker, jumping onto a crate and out of her reach. "What do you think you're doing?" Abu seconded the opinion from Aladdin's shoulder with screeches and gestures.

"Relax," Fatima said with an eye roll as she walked ahead of the group, her arms crossed and looking glum for someone finally sprung from a hot, crowded house after two days. "I'm just messing with you. What was Mukhtar whispering to you about in the shop?"

Aladdin's chest tightened. "He was just going over hand techniques for delivering the package." Aladdin pretended to hand something off to Abu. "Wanted to make sure I knew how to make the trade undetected."

Fatima didn't seem to buy it. "Well, if Mukhtar wants his newbie to deliver the package to Arif in a crowded market teeming with people, then I guess that's what he wants. Not my business."

Aladdin paled. *Well, when you put it that way . . .* he thought.

"But you're kind of making it your business," Kalila pointed out as she clanged cymbals together to the delight of a group of kids playing in the street. The children immediately started to follow them.

"Mukhtar isn't reckless. He must have a reason to have given Aladdin the job." Malik gave Aladdin a small smile. Fatima just huffed some more.

Aladdin ignored her. He was going to prove to Fatima that he could do this and that he belonged here. Part of him felt guilty, liking where he was so much when he still hadn't located Elham, but he couldn't help being mesmerized by this metropolitan city that he was starting to think of as his own. He clapped Malik on the back. "Thanks, Malik."

"You got it, and hey, look what else I've got?" He pulled a small loaf of bread out of his thawb and broke off half for Aladdin. "Never make a trade on an empty stomach if you can help it! I think that's a Mukhtarism, right?" He raced ahead to the others.

Aladdin laughed and broke off a piece for Abu, who chomped on his bread happily. Aladdin was about to take a piece himself, when he heard shuffling behind him.

Two small children were standing there with big, round eyes. They couldn't stop staring at the bread in Aladdin's hand. Abu grunted and held his own bread higher, as if he was afraid his piece was going to be stolen. Were these kids all alone? The boy reminded him of himself in some ways. Maybe it was the haircut. "You two all right?" Aladdin asked. "Need anything?"

The kids pushed in closer, not speaking. Aladdin could swear he heard one's stomach growl. *Share the wealth*, he remembered Elham saying when they passed around big bowls of food to eat in the caravan. Aladdin looked at the bread in his hand. He'd already eaten today. He wasn't working on an empty stomach. "Here," he said, holding out the half a loaf to the kids who looked at it longingly. "Take it.

It's yours." Abu grumbled for a moment before handing Aladdin his remaining piece as well. "We want you both to have it. We need to share, right?" The kids took the bread and ran off in a fit of giggles. Aladdin felt his heart soar. Elham would be proud of him.

"Aladdin! Stop moving like a camel!" Fatima shouted. "Let's go!"

Soon the group reached a crowded area of Agrabah. The market was near. Aladdin's pulse started to race. The sun was already lower in the sky — he was surprised Mukhtar let them set out so late in the day — and the relief of nightfall was around the corner. Twilight was already upon them. Something about the thought of stars soon appearing calmed his nerves. *The stars will always guide you*, he thought, thinking of Elham again.

First, he had to find Arif. Or was it the Night Bazaar? He still wasn't even sure how the Night Bazaar appeared. And how was he supposed to get away from the others if only one person could enter? What if Mukhtar was wrong and he wasn't worthy enough to get in? A million worries and questions ran through his mind. He heard Mukhtar's voice in his head. *Don't be swayed by things that seem too good to be true.* He felt his thawb pocket again to make sure the totem was still safe (it was) and thought about the totem — what did it do? What did Mukhtar's note say? He was dying to read it, but knew better than to take the totem out in broad daylight.

"Well, there's the fish market," Malik pointed out. "Do you see anyone who looks like this Arif guy Mukhtar wants you to meet?"

Aladdin looked around, not wanting to admit he'd failed to ask Mukhtar for a description. Would Arif just *know* who Aladdin was? There was certainly nothing about smelly fish that screamed *Night Bazaar*. "Not yet."

"Hmm . . . anyone else think Mukhtar is setting a trap?" Fatima smiled slyly. "Aladdin is new, so he's the one member of our crew who is dispensable."

Aladdin stiffened. Was that what Mukhtar was doing?

Kalila nudged Fatima's shoulder. "Don't say things like that!" Kalila looked at Aladdin apologetically as Fatima stepped away to examine a nearby stall. "Don't listen to her. She's just jealous. And protective. Mukhtar is the closest thing we have to a parent," she whispered. "She's just trying to keep him safe."

"I wouldn't do anything to hurt him," Aladdin vowed. "I want to do a good job, too."

"You will!" Kalila insisted. "Mukhtar giving you such a huge assignment is a big deal. It took months before he'd let me deliver anything on my own."

"Almost a year for me," Malik said as he backed into a peddler cart and sent apples rolling off it. "Sorry!" He rushed over to pick the apples up.

Aladdin noticed some of the other shopkeepers look over at the debacle and frown. This was not staying hidden. Fatima, seeing the commotion, motioned to them to follow her into a darkened alleyway. Aladdin stood with Abu on his shoulder, staring at shadows as they danced on the walls as nightfall set in.

"Sorry about that. Think the other shopkeepers are onto us now?" Malik whispered.

Aladdin peeked out of the alley to see if anyone was looking for them. He made eye contact with a shopkeeper and jumped. "Still watching."

Fatima yanked him back. "Don't look at them! Did they see you look at them?"

"No." Aladdin panicked. "I mean, I don't think so. Maybe."

She groaned.

"It's fine! I've still got the totem. See?" He lifted the griffin out to check that it hadn't been damaged during the walk — all that bouncing around! — and shifted it from one callused hand to the other, feeling the weight of it. He'd never held anything worth this much in his life, and he wasn't going to do anything to mess with Mukhtar's trust. The griffin's mouth opened unexpectedly and the jewels spilled out into his hand. Aladdin quickly pushed them back in.

"What are you doing? Don't take that out of your pocket!" Fatima gritted her teeth. "Have you learned nothing yet? We stay unseen and we never show off valuables."

"Relax," Kalila said soothingly, and turned to Fatima again. "So Malik knocked over some apples. It's not like we caused a scene, right? We've done nothing wrong."

There was a loud crunch.

The group turned to see Abu biting into a large red apple.

"Abu!" Aladdin scolded, and tried to grab what remained of the apple.

The monkey screeched and tried to turn away.

"A monkey running off with an apple is definitely a scene," Malik argued.

Fatima slapped her head. "Mukhtar told us to fly under the radar! Now all the shopkeepers have seen us. If you mess this job up, I'm not the one who is taking the fall for it. I earn my keep."

"That's what we all do," Kalila snapped.

"As soon as I have enough money, I'm out of here," Fatima said, crossing her arms and looking away.

"What does that mean?" Malik asked, looking at Kalila.

"Guys, remember that part about not causing a scene." The look in Malik's brown eyes was fearful as he peered out of the alley at the people walking by. "People can hear you."

"We need a distraction to get Aladdin back out there before Arif leaves," Kalila said. "What's our plan?"

Aladdin tried not to panic. *Please don't let me mess up this job before I've even started.* He closed his eyes and wished hard for a way out.

BOOM!

Aladdin's head turned with a jerk.

"What's that sound?" someone shouted.

"It's fireworks!" another yelled.

The kids looked at one another. Aladdin looked at Abu.

"Fireworks are the perfect distraction!" Malik said with glee. "Come on!"

The group rushed out of the alley. People everywhere were coming out of their homes and looking up from their place in the market to watch.

BOOM! KABOOM!

The darkening sky was exploding in light. Fireworks whizzed above them, washing the night sky in beautiful colors. Aladdin could stand and watch this all day, but he knew now was the time to move.

"What's the occasion for the fireworks?" a woman asked.

"The Sultan just announced a celebratory dinner for the new moon," a man told her. "The fireworks are to announce the dinner."

It was if the whole world was in a trance. Everyone moved in the direction of the fireworks, even Kalila, who forgot all about her conversation with Fatima—about anything they'd been talking about really—and followed the people down the street. Aladdin felt himself called to the fireworks, too, and started walking in that direction.

"Isn't that the boy who overturned your apple cart?" someone asked.

Aladdin turned around. It was the fruit vendor, and he was standing with some guards. His finger was pointed in their direction.

"Boy, we'd like to speak to you," said the vendor, walking toward him with the guards.

Aladdin froze.

"Abort mission. Scram!" Malik told the others. "Remember: Don't go home!"

Kalila, Malik, and Fatima took off in opposite directions as the fireworks continued to boom overhead, but Aladdin hesitated, his eyes still on the fish market. Arif. The Night Bazaar. He couldn't leave now. He had to stay in this square and get this totem to its final destination.

Abu let out a cry and dug his claws into Aladdin's shoulder blades as the vendor and guards drew closer.

"All right, Abu," Aladdin said, taking a deep breath as he weighed his options. "Left, we make our way into the street market, and right, we scatter." He bounced anxiously on his toes. Something told him not to run too soon. "What do you think, Abu? Which way do we go?"

"Stop! We just want to talk to you," one of the guards shouted as he got caught in the flow of people.

But what if the guard didn't want to just talk? What if he and the other guards detained him and that kept him from meeting up with Arif? Aladdin had no choice. He had to run. He dove into the crowd, heading back for the market. The crowd watching the fireworks was growing, making it impossible to maneuver around the courtyard, the people standing six deep, tightly clustered together like a vine, but Aladdin kept weaving.

BOOM! BOOM! BOOM!

"Wait!" the guard shouted again.

Aladdin panicked, getting all turned around in the chaos and not knowing which way to go. His friends were gone. The marketplace was so close he could smell it. There was still no sign of a hidden door or an entrance to a mysterious market or anyone named Arif. What was he going to do?

Aladdin . . .

His ears perked up. It was the voice again. The same voice he'd heard when he saw the bottle the day before. He could hear it as clear as he could hear the vendor and the guard shouting at him.

Aladdin, . . . here . . . we're right here. . . .

The voice was . . . magic.

Abu even gave a tiny chattering sound, growing restless.

"Do you hear it, too, Abu?" Aladdin asked his little friend. "Where is it coming from?"

"Stop right there!" the vendor called again, trying to push his way through a cluster of parents who were hoisting children high on their shoulders to see the colorful explosions. "We just have a question for you!"

Aladdin's window of opportunity to escape unseen was shrinking. Left, he went into the crowd and found what was hopefully the Night Bazaar. Right, he headed into the streets, avoiding going back to Mukhtar's. But if he went straight . . . he stared back at the alley from where he'd come.

That was interesting. Had it expanded? He remembered the pathway being tight and dark, but now it was growing brighter, a cloudy haze obscuring the path laid out in front of him, when before it had looked like a dead end.

Could this be the entrance to the Night Bazaar?

Aladdin looked around, his heart starting to beat faster.

Come, said the voice again, the haze from the alley almost looking like . . . no . . . it couldn't be — was that a finger drawing him near? *Come*.

Abu screeched worriedly.

"Boy! Wait!"

Aladdin whirled around. One of the guards had broken free of the pack and was feet away, his arms outstretched. There was no time to waffle.

"Choice made, Abu!" Aladdin said, leaping toward the alley, closing his eyes, and holding his breath as he imagined someone yanking him back.

But it didn't happen.

Aladdin didn't question his good fortune. He just kept running. Finally he opened his eyes. A smoky haze made it impossible to see anything in front of him, but when he turned around, he could see the fruit vendor and guards still standing in front of the alley.

"Where'd he go?" the guard asked.

"We need to find that boy," the vendor said. "If he wanted an apple, I would have given him one. I just wanted to talk to him first."

"Abu, they don't see us!" Aladdin didn't dare step any closer to the vendor or the guards, but he did wave his hands around. "Hello! Over here!" he said, much quieter than normal, but still enjoying himself.

The vendor and the guards still looked confused, peering at the alley strangely.

"Abu, they really can't see us!" Aladdin said in amazement, and Abu snickered. "Amazing what a little mist can do." Aladdin spun around, ready to move forward, and the mist thickened. He couldn't even see his hand in front of his face now. "Uh . . . that's a lot of smoke." Abu tried to cover Aladdin's eyes. "Abu! We're fine." He took a deep breath. "I know this is creepy, but water can't hurt anyone. The only way out is forward, so that's where we're going to go." Despite trying to sound brave, Aladdin found his legs slowing down while his heart beat faster as the tight alley seemed to continue to stretch out and widen.

The silence was so deep, all he was left with was his thoughts, and they turned to the only mother he'd ever known — Elham. *The stars will always guide you.* His heart felt a pang as he thought about Elham now. Were the Bedouin here in the city searching for him? Where did they go? How could he find them? He pictured Elham crying over him and he felt bad. If he could have one wish, he wished it could be to tell her he was okay. *Please, Elham, know I'm all right,* he thought as the alleyway stretched farther and farther until suddenly he found himself staring at a large structure. Abu screeched.

It was the largest tent Aladdin had ever seen.

Where did that come from? Aladdin wondered aloud. *Could this be the Night Bazaar?*

It certainly fit the description. The milky-white tent was so bright, it glowed like the moon, while a low-lying fog, much like the mist, nestled around it. And was it him, or did the moon look three times its normal size here? Wasn't the new moon still days away? Sayed Khalid charted such things and taught the Bedouin to do the same. And yet, here the moon was, seemingly coming closer and closer till it was hanging right over a tent that looked like none Aladdin had seen before. Abu clung to his shoulder as Aladdin walked over and realized the tent wasn't actually white at all — it was covered in hundreds of rugs, made of the finest silk he'd ever laid eyes on. This had to be the Night Bazaar. *I found the place, yes. But how do I know I'm going to be allowed inside?* Aladdin worried.

Come, Aladdin . . . Come inside! a voice beckoned.

And before he could even question what he was hearing, he saw a tent flap rise on its own, smoke unfurling from under it. Looking inside, Aladdin saw that it was too dark to see anything. His heart started to beat wildly again.

"I think the Night Bazaar is inviting us in!" he said, a mixture of awe and fear playing into his voice, which cracked. Mukhtar had been right — he'd been invited inside! Him! An orphan who was lost in an unusual city. The Night Bazaar wanted him to visit!

"Wait till Kalila, Fatima, and Malik hear about this," Aladdin whispered.

Like a moth to a flame, he ran fast, then faster, toward the darkened tent, dying to know what was waiting for him.

TWELVE

Aladdin pulled the tent flap out of the way and prepared to step inside. For a moment, it felt like the air pushed against him, trying to decide if he was actually worthy of entrance. Aladdin pushed harder against it and then, suddenly, he felt himself fly forward as if pushed from behind. Abu shrieked and held tight to Aladdin's neck, and Aladdin fell forward, righting himself before he hit the ground, which was covered in . . . stars?

Aladdin was certain that's what the luminescent glowing items were even though it seemed impossible. But there they were, both under the new sandals Mukhtar had given him and above his head, where the roof of the tent reflected a perfect evening sky dotted with even more stars. The moon was also visible. He stepped forward to find his footing and the mist parted, revealing several smaller tents inside the large one. The beautiful round tents with cut-outs that reminded him of the doors in Agrabah — intricately shaped and in bright, beautiful colors. They looked like the one at Mukhtar's shop, which also had an ornamental starry sky design above the door. It couldn't be a coincidence.

Mukhtar had visited the Night Bazaar, too, and honored the market-place with his door. Aladdin reached out to touch the doorframe.

"No touching!"

A man appeared out of the mist, standing with a long scroll that unwound behind him and trailed off into the darkness. The man's white beard was equally long, making his gray thawb look short by comparison even though it reached his bare feet.

"Greetings, Aladdin." The man's voice was worn like leather. "Welcome to your first Night Bazaar."

Aladdin stared at the man curiously. "How do you know my name?"

"I am Daa, the keeper of the bazaar, in a matter of speaking, and I decide who comes and who goes." He glanced over his scroll at Aladdin. "You were deemed worthy, so don't make me regret the decision. Only touch what you're going to buy, or use as a spell."

"Sorry, Daa," Aladdin said, looking at Abu unsurely. "Do you know where I can find . . . where I can find . . ." Why was he here? His brain felt like it was in a fog as thick as the mist outside the tent. He could vaguely recall being in the Night Bazaar for a reason, but he couldn't remember what that reason was.

"Don't tell me you forgot already!" Daa tsked. "This must be your first visit, so I'm happy to help you — to an extent. Don't want to lose your way or get stuck here. If you get stuck, we will put you to work — we always need more workers, especially ones that forget why they came and never ask to leave. Me? Personally?" Daa rambled on. "I'd love to leave someday and visit the mountains outside the city of Agrabah again, if even for a moment." He sighed. "Well, one can dream. So do you have a Night Bazaar destination in mind?"

Job! Aladdin already had a job, didn't he? He didn't want to stay in the Night Bazaar forever. He had somewhere to be. Aladdin racked his brain trying to remember where it was.

Job . . . job . . . job . . .

Abu whined in his ear, and he wasn't sure if the monkey was trying to tell him something or was as confused as he was. Aladdin tried to focus. What did Elham always say? "Get in touch with your heart by putting a hand on it so you remember." *Elham!* Elham and the Bedouin were his tribe, but now he had a new one and . . . What was this in his pocket? He started to pull out the totem, saw the statue, and stopped before the man could see what he was carrying! The thoughts rushed back to him . . . Mukhtar! Night Bazaar! Arif! Deliver the totem!

"I'm looking for someone named Arif," Aladdin said, feeling relieved. "I have to deliver a package to him."

"Aha, so you do remember, for now!" Daa's large, hazy blue eyes widened, and he clapped half heartedly. "Guess I'm never getting out of this joint because I can't find anyone new to take this job." Daa looked down at the unrolled parchment. "Arif . . . Arif . . . ah, yes, three tents down to the right. Or is it the left? I'm not sure. The Night Bazaar is a wondrous place, but be careful or you'll lose your way in here. It happens more often than you think. Focus."

Focus. He could do that. Focus on . . . Wait, what was he focusing on? Arif! Yes! He could do this. Find Arif. Then leave. No matter what wondrous things he saw. Three tents to the right . . . or the left. He could do this.

"We'll find it. Thank you, Daa," Aladdin said as he sidestepped the man and his scroll and headed to the first tent. Abu whined nervously from his shoulder. "Don't worry, buddy. We've got this. I hope."

Aladdin stepped inside and found a tent filled with large, inviting pillows illuminated by lanterns that cast shadows on the walls. The scent of the tent was sweet with a hint of spice and burning wood. Cardamom. The spice was from eastern lands, and Elham used the small bottle she had in her possession only rarely, saving it for medicinal purposes or occasionally cooking with it. But someone was using the spice here. He looked around the tent. There were lots of tiny spice bottles on crooked bookcases. The longer he lingered, the more he could smell other scents, too — vanilla, saffron, and nuts. And in the corner of the tent, a slight man no taller than Aladdin was using a mortar and a pestle to grind up cumin. A man stood in front of him, cloaked in darkness. Was one of them Arif? Aladdin tried to look busy picking up pillows to purchase while he listened to their conversation.

"How long is it going to take?" he heard the man at the counter say, sounding urgent.

The man grinding the spices reached for a bottle and dumped the contents into the stone mortar, then got to work again. "Patience, friend. This kind of spell takes time to prepare."

"I don't have time. I've searched years for this, and I'm not going to lose it now. I need that potion prepared immediately!"

"Potion?" Aladdin whispered to Abu. "I thought this shop was for spices." Abu seemed to bob his head in agreement.

"It will be done soon, my friend," said the shopkeeper. "Let me concentrate."

"Forget patience! And we aren't friends. I paid you handsomely. Now I want my potion already!"

"I just need to add one more ingredient and then we should let it sit for a while before it's used." The shopkeeper reached for a bottle on the highest shelf that was out of reach. The bottle floated down to his hand.

Aladdin's jaw dropped. Magick. Of course. They were in the Night Bazaar. Magick made sense in a magical tent, and yet he'd never seen magick at work before. Sure, the Night Bazaar itself had appeared out of nowhere, but this was magic right in front of his face and there was no denying it. He pressed himself into a corner, waiting to hear more. Something told him neither of these men was Arif.

"Fine, but you're sure this will work?" the man snapped. "I need there to be no question."

"If you do the spell right," the shopkeeper said patiently. "You remember what happened when you tried to do it before? It wiped out an entire city from existence."

"Yes, yes," the man said without a care in the world. "My mistake. The city was nothing much to begin with. So it disappeared? Not my loss."

Aladdin stiffened, dropping the pillow he was holding. A whole city could disappear because of a spell gone wrong?

"I have bigger plans than being sultan of one city," the man told the shopkeeper. "When I finally possess the power I'm after, I will rule the world."

The shopkeeper said nothing as three more bottles came gliding off shelves and flew across the tent. "Quite a goal, but let me remind you: Summoning involves concentration. If even the slightest change to this spell occurs, it could mean doom for you and everything that lives and breathes around you."

The man pounded his fist on the table, making Abu jump. "I am not a fool. I won't make the same mistake twice. I can handle this spell. And if something goes wrong, I don't care. This time, I have amassed enough protection charms to ensure I stay safe. I can't say the same for Agrabah, though. Not that I care much for this city anyway. Let it fall. Who will miss it? Perhaps my brother, who is hoping to be their next sultan, but not me."

Aladdin inhaled sharply as he stared at the green bottle that contained a spell dangerous enough that it could destroy a whole city if it was done wrong. No one should be allowed to cast a spell with dark magick like this. Aladdin needed to warn Mukhtar, Kalila, Malik, and Fatima.

"Well, if that's the case, could you at least warn Daa about when you plan on casting this spell? I'd like the Night Bazaar to move on before you casually use a potion that could destroy a city," said the shopkeeper sharply as he passed over the green bottle. "We've existed longer than your family line has been on this planet and we are meant to exist long after."

"Well, then the bazaar should be gone before the next new moon," said the cloaked figure. "It's long been prohesied that if the Cave of Wonders is going to open again, it will occur twelve years after the token was discovered under a new moon like the one soon to come to pass. Now I'm hearing that that token could be a diamond."

"There's not many diamonds to be found here," said the shop-keeper.

Aladdin stiffened. Mukhtar's note had mentioned a diamond being here in Agrabah, but he wouldn't say what it meant.

The man drummed his elegant fingers on the table and stared at the green bottle he'd just purchased. "I've done everything I could to track down the token — a charm — and be here in Agrabah ready for this moment, but I can't help but think . . ."

"Think what?" the shopkeeper pressed.

"That I'm missing something."

The shopkeeper nodded. "What you really need is a potion like this." He held up a yellow bottle that made a small tingling sound. "One that can show you the future. One that will let you know if all you're doing is worth the trouble and whether you will get all that you desire."

"Yesss . . ." the man hissed. "That's exactly what I want. Proof that

I will find the charm before the new moon! That I will receive great honor for accomplishing the mission my brother and the Azalam entrusted me with. That opening the Cave will make me more powerful than my brother or any sultan who walks this earth." He held out his hand. "I'll take the potion."

The shopkeeper smiled thinly. "Unfortunately, this is one of a kind and it's not for sale."

"Nonsense," said the man. "Everything is for sale. Name your price."

The shopkeeper stared at the yellow bottle in his hand unsurely. "I don't think I can part with it. It's said to be from the very cave you seek. And like many things in that cave, possessing it comes at a price. Knowing one's future can be quite dangerous. There can be cataclysmic results to knowing such a thing. It's part of the reason why I've never sold it. Plus, I've held on to it for centuries in case I ever needed to see the future myself."

"You wouldn't have told me about it if it weren't for sale," the man purred. "Name your price." The two continued to argue.

Aladdin couldn't stop staring at the yellow bottle. It appeared to glow in a way that made him sleepy. Why was he here again? Oh yes. To see Arif. But why? He thought for the moment then felt his pocket. The totem. He had to focus.

"Wow, Abu," Aladdin whispered. "Can you imagine one little potion showing you your destiny? Bet Mukhtar would be indebted to us forever if we brought him something like this. The shop would be so rich, we could buy our own palace."

Aladdin was talking so much, he didn't notice Abu climb off his shoulder and jump to a pillow beside them. Aladdin turned and saw the monkey's eyes trained on the yellow bottle, and he knew immediately what Abu was trying to do. As he reached his paws out to grab the bottle, Aladdin grabbed him and yanked him back. "Whoa! As much as I don't want this creepy guy getting his hand on either of these potions, we certainly can't afford to buy them ourselves. In fact, I don't think we should even touch something that dangerous."

Aladdin felt strange just being this close to such an item. His neck was actually starting to itch and warm, which was odd. He looked down at his charm, which seemed to be pulsing like a heartbeat. Now he was being silly. Charms didn't pulse. It had to be his nerves.

Abu frowned, then started chattering quietly — as if he was telling Aladdin off. While the move was kind of cute, it was also making it hard for Aladdin to hear what the men were saying. "Abu, I can't hear!"

But Abu wouldn't stop. His chatter moved to a high-powered shriek as he grew more indignant. Aladdin sensed what the monkey was thinking — the creepy guy shouldn't get to buy a potion that dangerous — but Abu was getting himself worked up over something neither he nor Aladdin could control. They were in the Night Bazaar to find . . . Arif. Yes, that was his name! And to . . . deliver a totem! That's it! He had to focus. But now Abu's little arms were flying. Before Aladdin could stop him, the monkey knocked over a bottle on the nearest shelf. It crashed to the ground and shattered.

The shopkeeper and the cloaked figure spun around.

THIRTEEN

MUKHTARISM NUMBER 27:
DON'T GET SLOPPY.

"Uh-oh," Aladdin whispered.

"Uh-oh," Abu repeated.

Aladdin did a double take. "Wait, you can talk?"

"You," the cloaked figure said softly, rushing toward Aladdin. "You look familiar." The rest of his face was still covered in shadows, but Aladdin got a good look at his eyes — they were cold as ice.

"Nope. I'm new here and clearly in the wrong tent. Sorry! Got to go." Aladdin reached for Abu, practically tripping over his own two feet as he backed out of the tent. Abu jumped to one of the bookshelves, and Aladdin scrambled to grab him. He could feel the heat rising on his neck but wasn't sure why.

The figure clutched his own chest. "You. Who are you?" he whispered, drawing near.

Go, Aladdin! a voice seemed to shout.

"Not without Abu!" Aladdin told the voice as the figure approached.

Aladdin could see he had two choices: dive out of the tent and get away or get to Abu and then find their way out together. Choice two was the riskier option, but he wasn't leaving without his new friend. The monkey had stuck by his side since Aladdin rescued him. Something told him they belonged together.

Aladdin thought fast. "I hate to mess up your tent, but . . ." He turned to the nearest bookshelf and sent it tumbling. Bottles went crashing to the floor.

"No!" the shopkeeper cried out, diving to the floor to pick up the bottles. "These potions can't mix, they'll — "

But his voice was swallowed up as a sizzling sound rose from the floor. Smoke unfurled from the spilled bottles, and there was a loud popping sound. It was like a million voices whispering at once, speaking in tongues Aladdin didn't understand. Were they saying enchantments? The shopkeeper dove out of the way, and Abu shrieked and jumped over the man's back, reaching for Aladdin, who caught the mischievous monkey in his arms.

"Wait! Stop!" the cloaked figure begged.

The sizzling and the voices grew louder. The sands shifted again, spiraling up into the air like a cyclone, forming what appeared to be a figure. Was that a tiger?

"Seek out the Diamond in the rough!" said a deep voice. Then the tiger roared and fell to the floor, returning to sand once more.

"*Diamond?*" the cloaked figure repeated, and his eyes locked on Aladdin's. He lunged.

Aladdin didn't hesitate. He held tight to Abu and practically dove out of the tent, rolling into a new tent. Was this tent two? Tent three? Had they gone left? Right? Why was he here again? *Arif!* Aladdin reminded himself, his heart beating wildly. There was something about that man that made him want to run and never look back. Mukhtar had talked about dangerous magic before and this was clearly it. Aladdin didn't want to be anywhere near it. He turned around, sensing the man near, but the tent they'd just been in had vanished.

Aladdin breathed heavily. "I don't know about you, Abu, but this Night Bazaar isn't feeling so magical anymore." Abu chattered nervously, looking around.

The shadows in this tent moved along the walls from a lone candle flickering in the darkness. Aladdin could feel the hair on his arms stand up. There was something about the air in this tent that he didn't like. It was thicker and stale, as if whatever was in this tent had been locked up for a long time.

Suddenly a flame shot up in the corner of the tent. Aladdin could swear the flickers had eyes. All around him, he heard whispering and deals being made in shadows but saw no one present. How could he hear people but not see them?

"I don't think Arif is in here, Abu. Let's go," Aladdin whispered, backing up. He bumped into something large — or was it some*one*?

"Hello," a woman hissed, her face shrouded by her hood. "You're new, aren't you?" she said, her tone softening. "What are you here to sell, or is it buy?"

"New? I'm old. *Older*." Aladdin stumbled over his words. "And very late. Got to go." He banged into something hard and realized there was nothing but empty space in front of him. Huh?

"See anything you like here?" the woman asked. "There's power in this room if you give me what I want in return. I know plenty who would pay to know the Diamond in the rough is in the Night Bazaar. . . ."

Aladdin froze. *Diamond*. "No diamonds here. I'd love a date, though. Or a drumstick. We're kind of hungry, right, Abu? We should get home for supper."

"Pity," the woman said. "There's much I could tell you if you had time to listen for a thousand years." She started to laugh, the sound so loud it practically burst Aladdin's eardrums.

A thousand years? Aladdin spun around looking for a way out when there had been none before. He clutched his charm for good luck. *Please*, he thought. *Help me find Arif!*

The tent suddenly opened, and Aladdin and Abu fell through, but this time there was no ground to stop them. Aladdin felt himself and Abu free fall into nothingness, screaming all the way.

Aladdin reached out for something — anything to grab on to and break their fall, but there was nothing there. Abu was screeching as loudly as he could, and all Aladdin could think about was how he didn't want them both to end up like squashed bugs. Mukhtar wouldn't know what happened to him. Neither would Elham . . . yes, Elham! He remembered her name. And Arif's! And the totem! But focusing wouldn't save him. He had no magic genie or a lamp at his disposal. The only person who could help him now was himself. Aladdin thought of the charm around his neck and shouted at the top of his lungs, "STOP!"

He and Abu froze in midair.

Aladdin looked down. Below him was a third tent. Even in midair, he could feel the warmth bouncing off it and heard laughter inside. Unlike the other two tents, which were shrouded in mystery and involved people he wasn't sure he could — or should — trust, this tent felt right. Was that where Arif was hiding?

"Abu, I think we've found the right tent . . . if only we could float down to it. Have any thoughts?"

Abu started to chatter again, making wild hand motions and looking like he was trying to mime something about drinking.

"Are you thirsty? We will get you something to drink when we get out of here. I'm not sure I'd trust anything we find in the Night Bazaar. But first: Let's get back on the ground."

And just like that, they started to float down, past the roof of the tent and landing on a soft bed of stars.

"Looks like someone in this bazaar wants us to enter this third tent," Aladdin said. Was it Daa? Or someone else? He looked around the sides, trying to find a flap to pull to enter. "If only I could find a way in."

"There you are," said a man, appearing at an opening in the tent, his brown eyes and smile warm and inviting. "We've been waiting for you."

"We?" Aladdin asked.

The man nodded and smiled. "Yes. Myself and Arif."

FOURTEEN

"Arif." Aladdin gaped. "You know Arif of Agrabah?"

The man motioned inside the tent again. "Right this way, Aladdin. Daa told us you'd be coming. You've passed the test and he's ready to meet you."

"Test?" Even Abu cocked his head in confusion. "You mean surviving the first two tents was a test? I wish someone had told me that."

Aladdin was too curious not to follow. Thankfully this tent wasn't like the others. The air smelled sweet, like honey, and the lanterns cast no shadows on the brightly colored tent walls. Instead, there were numerous multicolored rugs. Soft music played from an oud that had no player, and candles seemed to dance and move through the air around the tent, but Aladdin didn't feel afraid. He felt like this was the tent he was meant to be in all along. There were plush pillows aplenty and more fruit and bread on platters than he ever thought was possible at a meal. Abu saw the grapes and started to salivate.

"Take whatever you like to eat and drink," the man said. "It's safe. I promise. I'll find Arif."

Abu didn't hesitate even after Aladdin's warning. He jumped off Aladdin's back and landed next to a platter of food, taking the largest piece of bread he could find and chomping into it.

"Abu, what did I just say?" Aladdin started to scold him, but then he realized they were alone once more. "Where did he go?"

A new table appeared, covered with jewels and trinkets. The display reminded him of the wares in Mukhtar's shop. There was everything from small totems to gemmed plates and from mirrors to jewelry. Abu's eyes widened.

"Oooh!" he screeched, dropping his bread, his eyes growing three times their usual size as he picked up a jeweled crown and tried to put it on. The crown was so large it slipped right over him. Aladdin laughed and swooped in to help.

"He said you could take some food, not jewels, although this is pretty nice," Aladdin admitted as he lifted the crown off Abu and turned it over in his hands.

Abu squeaked and tried to pry the crown back out of Aladdin's hands, but Aladdin held firm.

"Abu!" Aladdin scolded. "We're here to see Arif and get out of here without any more trouble." He looked behind him. "Do you want to run into that cloaked man from the first tent again? There was something about the way he looked at me that I didn't like." Aladdin shuddered and placed the crown back on the pile of trinkets. "You heard Daa earlier. I think this Night Bazaar is making me lose my mind. I have to stay focused — Mukhtar, Arif, deliver the totem, and leave. If we do that, we'll be okay." He stared up at the tent ceiling, which looked just like a starry night. "I don't know, Abu. Was coming here the right idea? I want to make Mukhtar happy, but everything is changing so fast the last few days. I lost the Bedouin. I gained you and the others. What if I can't cut it here and I lose you guys, too?"

Abu grunted angrily as if Aladdin was bananas to think that.

"I know, we're a team. I just don't want to mess up again." Aladdin thought about losing Elham after wandering away from the market-place again, and his stomach twisted. "I just want to find someplace I can stay for good. I want a home, and if there's one in Agrabah like I think there is, I want to earn my keep and do what Mukhtar asked me to do tonight. I don't know why I'm telling you all this. . . ."

Abu hopped back onto Aladdin's shoulder, nuzzling his neck.

"I guess you feel the same way, huh, buddy?" Aladdin scratched the monkey's back. "You're kind of an orphan, too." Abu made a small grunting sound. "Guess it's good we found each other."

Abu screeched happily.

"Aladdin."

At the sound of the man's voice, he spun around. The man had some-one with him who was only a few years older than himself. A bead of sweat was falling from the younger man's brows and his hair was matted to his head as if he'd labored in the heat. Aladdin knew the feeling.

Aladdin stepped forward. "Arif?"

The young man nodded. "Mukhtar said you were coming, but when I didn't see you earlier, I thought you didn't make it here." He smiled. "But here you are."

"So you work in the fish market and at the bazaar?" Aladdin was confused.

Arif laughed and looked at his companion. "Even a Night Bazaar needs fish. I work here, but yes, I can see what happens in Agrabah, too. We've been watching you since you arrived, Aladdin."

"Me?" Aladdin pointed to himself. "Why? I'm nobody."

"Nobody you are not," Arif said simply. "You are special, even if you can't see that yet. That's why it's our job to keep you safe. Did you bring Mukhtar's message?"

Me? Safe? Aladdin didn't understand. He reached into his pocket and pulled out the griffin.

The whites of Arif's eyes grew large.

Aladdin held tight to the totem. "I was told you had something for Mukhtar as well."

Arif nodded and looked around worriedly. "I could be killed for this. The Azalam has eyes everywhere."

Aladdin stiffened. "The Azalam?" They were the ones Elham swore had run into Aladdin's parents and left him to die alone when he was a baby. He felt his whole body flush with anger.

Arif whispered, "We must be quick. If they find out what I've told you . . ."

"They won't," said the man next to him kindly. "You know this is what must be done. The Night Bazaar wants to protect the Diamond, too."

"They don't even know about the Diamond," Arif insisted, talking to him instead of to Aladdin.

"But they will," the man insisted. "They're close to finding out before the new moon. We have to stop them." He eyed Aladdin and smiled again. "This one holds promise. I can feel it."

Arif looked at Aladdin again. "You said that about the last one and the one before that and the one a hundred times before. These Diamonds . . ."

"But this one is the Diamond in the rough," the man said. "There is a difference. He will be ready."

"Maybe not today," Arif huffed.

"Someday. Either way, he could be the one who keeps the Cave safe for another thousand years," the man added.

What were they talking about? Aladdin wondered. This diamond business made no sense, but Aladdin knew if Arif had information to get to Mukhtar, he couldn't leave without it. He couldn't let the Azalam hurt anyone else. "You can trust me," he said, thinking of Kalila telling him the very same thing when they first met. "I am fast and you can tell Daa I am ready to leave the bazaar, as magical as it was to see it in action. I will get it to Mukhtar and make sure no one else sees it. Promise."

Arif looked at the man with him then back at Aladdin and held out his hand to make the trade. Aladdin handed over the statue and Arif handed him . . .

"A note?" Aladdin grumbled. He was trading a priceless totem and jewels for a piece of paper? Was this a trick?

"This has all the information Mukhtar needs," Arif said as the tent around them waffled.

Abu saw the table of gems fading away and scrambled to grab the crown, but the table was gone in an instant.

"Get him that message." Arif's voice penetrated the air before he and his companion turned to mist. "Go quickly, before he catches you, Aladdin."

"Who catches me?" Aladdin wondered aloud as they disappeared before his eyes and the tent along with them.

"Goodbye, Aladdin!" came a voice that sounded like Daa's. "Sorry you won't be staying with us. Do visit again! And good luck!"

Smoke began to swirl around Aladdin's feet and he groaned. Was he about to free fall again? "Not again."

Abu screeched and hopped back up on Aladdin's shoulders as a mist appeared, thickening around them. The starry night sky that acted as the larger tent's ceiling faded away, too. In its place, Aladdin could just make out the outline of the alley from which he'd originally come. He could hear shouting again, too. It was the shopkeepers again, and they were still looking for him. Aladdin shoved the paper in his pocket and tried to figure out his escape plan. Spinning around, he collided with another man and stumbled backward.

"There you are!" It was the man in the cloak from the spice shop. The one who said that the potion, if done incorrectly, could destroy Agrabah. "Get over here, boy!"

The wind picked up around Aladdin and his hair stood on end.

Run, a voice in his head said. *Run!*

"Sorry! Got to go!" Aladdin scrambled to get out of the man's path, walking as quickly as he could to get away, but the mist around Abu and him was thickening and he couldn't tell his left from his right.

"I know you . . . I can feel it. . . ." the man said, his voice urgent as he ran after him. "There's something about you . . . I can't put my finger on it, but I know you!"

"We definitely don't know each other. I can promise you that!" Aladdin said, and that's when he felt the heat rising from his neck. Abu started chattering, jumping up and down, and practically falling off his shoulder as he pointed to Aladdin's necklace. It was glowing.

The hooded figure gasped and reached out for the beetle around Aladdin's neck. "The charm," he whispered reverently. "You have it? But how?" His eyes narrowed. "Give it to me, boy. That belongs to the Azalam!" He swiped at Aladdin's neck.

The Azalam? No. That was impossible! Through the mist, Aladdin noticed something strange. The hooded figure's neck was glowing, too. He squinted to see what the man had around his neck. Was that a golden half of a beetle? Aladdin gasped. Was this charm and the one Aladdin had connected somehow?

"This is mine," Aladdin said, feeling shaky. "And unlike in the spice shop, it is really not for sale." He started to run.

"No! Stop! I will pay any price, boy. ANY PRICE!"

Aladdin stumbled over a barrel in the alley, almost sending Abu flying, but he scrambled to his feet and kept running. He was not selling this man his necklace. He'd almost parted with it once this week when he thought he'd have to give it to Mukhtar as payment. He wasn't doing that again. But he wasn't quick enough. The cloaked man grabbed hold of the back of his thawb. Abu squeaked.

"That charm is mine! Give it to me!" the man shouted.

"No!" Aladdin cried. The man grabbed hold of Aladdin's wrists, and the two found themselves struggling as Abu jumped from Aladdin's shoulder to the ground to flee. Both of their necks were glowing. Aladdin felt the heat of his own charm practically burning into his chest, but he wouldn't stop trying to get away. For a moment, he thought he was doomed. Then, suddenly, something went flying past Aladdin's face, hitting the man.

"OW!" the man cried, holding his face and stumbling backward, where he got hit with something else. "OW!" The man went down hard.

Aladdin looked up. The mist had finally started to clear, and he could see Abu was standing on a crate stacked behind them. He was throwing rocks as hard as he could. "Nice, Abu!"

Aladdin heard a groan and looked down at the cloaked figure. His hood had fallen away and Aladdin could see his face. He inhaled sharply. "You're the grand vizier," Aladdin whispered before he could think better of it.

The man's eyes locked on Aladdin's, then looked down at the glowing charm around his neck again.

Aladdin didn't hesitate. He grabbed Abu, placed him on his shoulder, then turned and ran away from the man, away from the Night Bazaar. But he wasn't far away enough that he couldn't hear the grand vizier shouting to him.

"You can't hide, boy! I'll find you! I won't stop till I find you!"

FIFTEEN

I'll find you.

As they wound their way through darkened, quiet streets, the words echoed in Aladdin's ears. Abu was silent, watching Aladdin and waiting for him to say something to explain what had just happened. But Aladdin didn't understand it any more than Abu did — why did the grand vizier have the same charm as he did? *Were* they two halves of a whole? Both charms were glowing so bright it was hard to make out what the grand vizier's actually looked like, but it sort of looked like a beetle. It was clear both charms were connected somehow.

Aladdin's parents had been killed by the Azalam, leaving behind only their child and this charm. If the charm was important, why hadn't the Azalam taken it from him? Was the grand vizier working with the Azalam? Aladdin could have sworn he'd heard him mention them in the spice tent. Why would the Azalam have one half of this charm and an orphan have the other?

Nothing made sense except that the grand vizier was dangerous.

All he cared about was getting what he wanted. Not what was good for Agrabah. And what exactly was supposed to happen the night of the next new moon? He'd find a cave? Aladdin didn't understand anything he'd heard. Especially all that diamond-in-the-rough business.

Aladdin stared up at the night sky and thought of Elham again. He took a deep breath and remembered her words: *When all is lost, look to the stars.* He knew Elham didn't mean it literally — she wasn't a magician. Spending so much time outside, he knew she looked to the sky to feel calm. But when he did the same now, he just felt lost.

And yet he wasn't really. When he looked down, he realized his feet had taken him straight to Mukhtar's street without his ever realizing it. His head might have still been foggy from his time in the Night Bazaar, but his body knew where home was — Mukhtar's shop here in Agrabah.

Abu grunted again and clung to Aladdin's neck so tight, Aladdin couldn't breathe.

"Abu! It's okay," Aladdin promised. "We're safe. He can't find us. . . ." He glanced back at the way they came. "I hope." Abu whined some more. "In fact, maybe we should just leave this grand vizier business out of our conversation with the others, you know? The important thing is we got the message to Arif and Arif got his reply to Mukhtar. Let's let Mukhtar take care of things. There's nothing for us to worry about." Even as he said the words aloud, Aladdin worried he was wrong.

Abu ran a paw over his head and chattered on, his eyes even wider than before. And that's when Aladdin realized . . . the monkey looked guilty.

"Abu?" Aladdin warned. "Is there something you want to tell me?"

Abu gulped hard and pulled off his fez, retrieving the priceless yellow bottle. The potion that allowed someone to see the future.

Aladdin closed his eyes tight and thought he could hear the bottle whispering to him, begging to be opened. "Abu!" Aladdin jumped. "That bottle wasn't for sale for a reason — it's dangerous. Didn't you hear the shopkeeper? And if the grand vizier knows it's missing, that's even more of a reason to come looking for us!" Abu squeaked apologetically. "What were you thinking?"

Abu chattered on incessantly, alternating between high-pitched squeals and apologetic grunts. Aladdin could swear he understood the point Abu was trying to make. A bottle like this was valuable. People would pay top dollar to have a potion that would tell them the future. And that's why Abu had wanted it — *at first*. But he also knew a potion this dangerous in the wrong hands — like the grand vizier's — it could mean big trouble. So Abu took it, thinking it was better off with him and Aladdin, but now he was terrified to even have the thing on him. When Abu was finished gesturing and squeaking, he stared at Aladdin mournfully. His expression made Aladdin think the monkey was trying to say: *Are you going to ditch me now, too?*

Being left behind was Aladdin's fear now, too. He didn't want Abu to feel that way. He held out his arm for the monkey to climb onto. "Let's get one thing straight: You and I are a team. You made a mistake. I'm not leaving you because of it. We'll fix this problem. Together."

The monkey jumped from the crate to Aladdin's arms and hugged him. The two were quiet for a moment.

"Now the question is: What do we do with this thing?" Aladdin stared at the bottle in Abu's paws. "We can't just toss it. If someone found it, it could be dangerous." Abu nodded his head furiously in agreement. "But if we hold on to it and the grand vizier comes looking for it and finds us..." Aladdin shook his head now, too. "But we can't tell Mukhtar, either, can we? If he finds out we stole something from the Night Bazaar, he might want us to leave the shop." The thought of him and Abu out on his own was enough to make him abandon that plan.

He looked over his shoulder, half expecting Daa and the Bazaar to appear out of nowhere and demand the bottle back. "For now, let's just keep this between us."

Abu screeched in agreement and offered Aladdin the potion. Aladdin took the bottle and placed it in his pants pocket, praying no one would find it.

Aladdin was never so happy to see Mukhtar's door. He was surprised to find it wide open. He heard voices inside and rushed in, stopping short as soon as he entered. Abu screeched.

"What happened?" Aladdin said, aghast.

The shop had been ransacked. Every shelf lay bare, smashed items littered the floor, and the large mirror that had started to desilver had a crack across its middle. Kalila, Fatima, Mukhtar, and Malik stood among the ruins.

"Aladdin!" Kalila threw her arms around him. "We thought they had you!"

Aladdin stiffened, thinking of the grand vizier, who worked for the Azalam. He shook his head. He was making himself mad. "Who? The guards? No, Abu and I gave them chase, but we got away. They kept saying they wanted to talk to me, but I was afraid, so I kept going."

"Yeah, well, someone chased you right here!" Fatima grumbled. "Don't you remember the rules? Run and hide! Someone tore this place apart, and I'm sure it was because they were looking for you."

"Me? But I didn't come back here till now," Aladdin swore even as his heart began to pound again. Had the grand vizier found him already?

"Fatima, let's not get ahead of ourselves," said Mukhtar, sounding calm. "Three shops were hit on this very street. It appears to be a random robbery and no one was here when it happened, thank the stars. It doesn't even look like they took anything." He looked at Aladdin. "You okay, Al? You look shook up."

"I'm all right." Aladdin swallowed hard, and his hand brushed against the pocket holding the potion. He could feel the bottle practically calling to him, begging to be opened. But that was silly. These thoughts were all in his head. "But the shop . . . I'm so sorry."

"Did you make the trade?" Mukhtar asked, his eyes questioning.

The rest of the kids looked at Aladdin. Kalila seemed hopeful while Fatima was still mutinous. *I'll find you.* Aladdin pushed thoughts of the grand vizier aside and stared triumphantly at Fatima. "Yes I did. Arif gave me this to give to you." He reached into his other pocket and pulled out the small piece of paper.

"Good job, Aladdin!" Malik said, clapping him on the back. "The Mukhtarisms worked. Your first job was a success!"

Kalila whistled with approval, and Abu squeaked happily. "I knew you could pull it off."

Mukhtar exhaled loudly. "Good job, kid." He placed the paper in his pocket without reading it. "Real good."

"*Good?* Look what happened here!" Fatima's face reddened. "You gave him one assignment and the shop gets ransacked. That's never happened before." She shook her head at Aladdin. "Which way did you run? We didn't see you anywhere."

Aladdin's eyes shifted back and forth from Kalila to Mukhtar. He sensed he wasn't supposed to tell the others about the Night Bazaar, but he couldn't keep lying.

I'll find you.

Aladdin looked at Abu, who started to whistle and looked up at the ceiling. "I don't know. I just ran. I didn't see you guys anywhere and we got turned around in an alley. Then we ducked inside somewhere till the coast was clear."

I'll find you. I'll find you.

Aladdin closed his eyes, trying to block out the grand vizier's voice.

What if his men already knew how to find him and they'd tracked him down to Mukhtar's? Would they come back for the potion?

"Al, you okay?" Malik asked gently.

It was the first time Malik had called him Al. "Yeah! I, uh, just trying to remember what the street I was on looked like, but if you've seen one spice shop, you've seen them all. Am I right?" He nudged Abu, who started to laugh along with him. The others just stared at them.

"The important thing is you're safe," Mukhtar said. "And nothing of value was taken here. It looks worse than it is. You think I keep the good magick items out front? No. I'm smart. I keep the junk out here." He patted Aladdin's arm and looked at Fatima. "Give Aladdin a break."

Fatima stared at him suspiciously. "I feel like he's hiding something. He's all green and sweaty."

Sweaty? Was he sweaty? He felt his forehead. Yes, he was sweaty. But that didn't prove anything. He did feel a little green, though. "I'm not," Aladdin said, but his voice cracked.

"He's lying!" Fatima insisted.

Mukhtar frowned. "Aladdin, did something happen when you delivered the message?"

I'll find you. Again he wondered if the grand vizier already had found him. He felt his breathing grow rapid in panic, but he couldn't say anything in front of the others without revealing the existence of the Night Bazaar, too. He had to think. "Everything went great," Aladdin insisted. "I made the trade. I gave you the message. That's all." His voice cracked again.

"You are hiding something!" Fatima said again.

Mukhtar put a hand on Aladdin's shoulder. "Are you sure there's nothing else you want to tell us?"

"I'm just tired." Aladdin's heart beat faster. He was in too deep now. He couldn't mention the potion even if he wanted to.

Fatima looked at Mukhtar. "I told you taking on another kid wasn't a good idea. It hasn't even been a week and look what's happened."

"Fatima, enough! Stop blaming Aladdin," Kalila snapped.

"Yeah, Fatima," Malik agreed. "What is your problem?"

"Mind your own business, Malik!" Fatima fumed. "My problem is we never fought like this before *he* arrived."

"We're only fighting because you're starting up with Aladdin," Malik countered.

Everyone started to bicker at once.

"Enough! Everyone!" Mukhtar told them. "Let's clean up this mess. We have a shop to reopen tomorrow morning at dawn. You too, Abu."

Abu rolled his eyes and sputtered, clearly annoyed, but Aladdin grabbed a broom and started sweeping. Mukhtar stopped him.

"Not you," Mukhtar said. "You and I are going to have a private chat."

SIXTEEN

NASIR

By the time Nasir had returned to the palace, he was in a fit of rage. The new moon was only a few days' away and he'd been so close to getting the other half of the charm!

"That stupid boy!" Nasir seethed, picking up a vase and sending it flying across the room. It hit a birdcage that had just arrived that afternoon.

"Squawk! Squawk! Stupid boy! Stupid boy!"

Nasir groaned. His brother's macaw, Iago, had been sent to Agrabah as a "gift" to keep Nasir company. At least that's what his brother claimed, but Nasir knew the real reason he had been strapped with Iago — the bird was a spy. It sounded crazy, Nasir knew, but his brother loved that dreadful macaw more than he loved the Azalam or his family, and he trusted the bird above all others. Even his only brother. The bird was there to make sure Nasir got the job done.

Don't disappoint me, Nasir, he remembered his brother threatening. *Find the other half of the charm or don't return.*

Older than Nasir by eighteen months, his brother had always

thought himself king of the palace, even if their family was rarely invited onto the palace grounds. His brother was a lowly sorcerer like the rest of their family, kept around by the Azalam for their power to conjure certain potions and charms. (Unlike Nasir, he never focused on any that would benefit himself. There was nothing wrong with beauty tonics, but Nasir's brother couldn't care less about those things.) The one thing he did agree with his brother on was that their lot in life was wrong. *We are meant for great things, Nasir. I am meant to rule and you will be at my side and should act accordingly.* He was the one who had kept them in the Azalam's good graces all these years, summoning the beetle charm he wore around his neck. Sure, it had been broken in half, but half was a start. They'd searched over ten years for the other piece of the charm and never found it . . . until now.

What was a common boy doing with a charm that powerful? Did the boy have any clue what he had in his possession? Perhaps. Nasir had found the child in the Night Bazaar, of all places. He had to be someone who could get inside.

Why had he let that monkey get the better of him and allowed the child to get away?

"AAAAHHH!" Nasir shouted in frustration, tossing another vase across the room, then three bottles sitting on the table in the center of his living space.

"Squawk! Squawk! Aaah!" Iago said, flapping his red wings and sending feathers flying.

But Nasir didn't care who heard him. That boy had the other half of the beetle he'd been searching for forever. He knew it was here in Agrabah. His brother did, too, and Nasir swore he would get past the Sultan so he could search for it and then bring it back to his brother to . . . to what? Let his brother claim the glory? Open the Cave on his own? Nasir shook the thought from his mind. Right now he had to focus on getting that charm back.

When he'd gone in search of the Night Bazaar earlier that evening, he'd doubled down on his luck by sending some of his own men to ransack area junk shops to see if any were in possession of the beetle and unaware of its worth. They'd turned up nothing. But that was because the boy had been in the Night Bazaar! He knew who had the charm now! He just had to find the boy.

When Nasir returned from the Night Bazaar, he'd given Faaris the description of the boy with the charm and sent him to try to find out who the child was. Now Faaris was taking impossibly long getting back to him with answers. What had it been? An hour?

There was a knocking at the door. It was about time! Nasir went to the door and threw it open. "Well?"

Faaris looked worried. "I asked everyone, sir, but the description of the boy was rather vague. There are hundreds of children who could look like him."

"But are all those children wearing necklaces with this charm?" Nasir asked, holding up his own necklace. He had half a beetle around his neck, as if the insect had been cut straight down the middle. His half gleamed in the moonlight filtering through the balcony.

"Beetle! Squawk!" Iago parroted.

"Yes, beetle," Nasir corrected himself. Maybe this macaw would be more helpful than he thought if it could recognize Nasir's charm.

Faaris blinked. "But, sir, this city is large. Am I supposed to stop at every home and question people about their children? Won't they be suspicious?"

Nasir felt his frustration grow. "I don't care! Just find that child!" His brother was the one who'd had a vision of the Cave of Wonders opening this year, during a summer new moon, when spells were more powerful. That date was fast approaching. Nasir needed that charm to open the Cave and fulfill his destiny. He snapped his fingers trying to think of more details he could share. "Oh! He's got a pet monkey who doesn't leave his side. That should help you. Search the marketplace — I am sure a street rat like him works there. And don't return till you find him!"

"But, sir — the dinner is only a few days away. The Sultan has given us much to do to get ready." Faaris seemed to hesitate, stepping back a few feet. "Are you sure we should be worried about finding some boy?"

"YES!" Nasir boomed. "This boy is the key to everything! You understand me? He must be found! Let me worry about what's left to be done for the dinner." He'd push everything off till the last minute, then assign others to finish up. "Just find the boy!" He slammed the door in Faaris's face and placed his head in his hands. He groaned. "He will never find that boy."

"*Squawk! Never find! Never find!*" Iago agreed.

"If only I hadn't used the last of my locator potions to find Agrabah!" It hadn't helped that his exit from the spice shop at the Night Bazaar had been hasty. The shopkeeper was so angry about losing the future casting spell, he'd banished Nasir from even negotiating with him after that. "How could I have let that child get away?" Nasir asked Iago, even if the bird couldn't understand. In anger, he threw two more bottles, not realizing till it was too late that one was a potion he used in many important spells. "No!" Nasir cried as the bottle flew across the room, smashing into Iago's cage and spilling its contents.

Smoke from the potion rose in a cloud through the cage bars, enveloping the macaw before Nasir reached him.

"*Squawk! Squawk!*" Iago panicked.

All Nasir could think was what he would tell his brother if the darn bird died by accidental poisoning. Which bottle had he thrown?

Iago was frantic now, flying up and down in the tight cage, feathers flying everywhere, sounding like he was choking. Nasir wasn't sure what to do.

If the thing died, maybe his brother wouldn't notice a replacement. Who was he kidding? His brother would notice a replacement.

The bird kept squawking, his coughing getting louder and louder. Nasir neared the cage, not helping, not hindering the bird, just watching in fascination as the smoke around it faded away and the bird finally stopped flapping. He seemed to suddenly look right at Nasir, which was unnerving.

"*Squawk! Squawk! Squawk* — UGH! What was in that thing? It smelled atrocious."

Nasir gasped. "You can talk?"

Iago raised one of his eyebrows at him. "No, I'm just pretending, you second-rate sorcerer. Why Jafar didn't just come on this trek himself instead of sending a vain hothead like you I'll never know."

Nasir grew enraged. "I am not a hothead!" He grabbed the bars of the cage. "How are you able to talk to me all of a sudden?"

The bird's eyes widened. "Wait. You can understand me? Must have been that potion you threw at my head!"

"The truth serum. Of course. Now I can hear your every thought."

Iago went to his water dish and took a drink. "Dreadful. Could you please have that servant of yours refill this thing with clean water at least three times a day? How hard is it to remember to give a bird decent water? You're always wasting so much of it with your multiple daily baths." He shook his head.

Nasir was in awe. "That potion has taken your primitive mimicking abilities and turned them into a proper person's speech. It's like you're human." He walked around the cage, staring at the macaw. "Fascinating."

"You know what's fascinating? Being stuck in a cage all day — not. *Squawk!* Let me out already, will you?"

Nasir paused.

Iago rolled his eyes. "Oh, come on, already. We both know why I'm here — to make sure you get the job done — and I can do that from this cage or I can actually help you track down the amulet you let slip through your hands. Yes, I heard you lament about the whole thing. And ask Faaris to locate the boy who had it on. Even when I couldn't talk, I could understand you." The bird looked him straight in the eyes. "You're never going to find that kid, by the way. You're not being smart enough."

"How dare you!" Nasir seethed.

"Relax. I am trying to tell you Faaris won't be able to find him. See one street rat, you've seen them all, you know? If you want to find that kid, you need to find out what he was doing in the Night Bazaar to begin with. Who was he meeting with? Couldn't have been an accident he was attending a magical shopping market, could it?"

Nasir stopped seething and thought for a moment. "You make a good point, Iago."

"I know I do. We need to find the guy who gave him entrance."

"Daa," Nasir said suddenly. "The man who gives entrance to the Night Bazaar is Daa. I've dealt with him many times before."

"Go see Daa — you're obviously worthy of entrance, get him to tell you the name of the kid he saw tonight and where he was headed. You can threaten him if you have to — and then you'll know where this brat lives."

Nasir hated that the bird was right (even if he was also mildly impressed. Not that he'd tell Iago that). "Of course that's what I'm going to do." He grabbed some jewels and things to barter with — they were worthless compared to opening the Cave — and prepared to head out. "I'm the one who tracked the charm to this city in the first place! Not my brother. I can get Daa to give me what I need. The charm is here. Soon I will get my hands on it and my destiny will be fulfilled!"

"You mean, your brother's destiny, right?" Iago asked, sounding extremely smug.

Darn bird! "Yes. Of course, my brother." Nasir's voice was dry. "I'm just so happy for him."

He could tell Iago wasn't convinced. He didn't blame him. The truth was since Nasir had arrived in Agrabah and come so close to holding the other half of the beetle in his own two hands, he'd made a decision: Why return to the Azalam or his annoying older brother and hand over what he'd found on his own? This mythical Cave of Wonders, whatever it was, and its riches could be his. He'd become so powerful there would be no one to stop him. Certainly not a macaw. Still, maybe it was best to make Iago think otherwise. He didn't want the bird flying off to tattle on him to his brother. "But maybe there is something in it for you, too, for your loyalty," Nasir said. "We both deserve something after putting up with having to stay in such a lowly city."

"I'll say," Iago agreed. "Can you believe this dump only has a single palace we all have to share? Pitiful. The Azalam at least know how to make themselves feel comfortable at home."

Nasir opened the cage and Iago stared out with interest. "While we're stuck here, there is no reason why we shouldn't enjoy this palace together. All I ask is that you don't return to my brother to give him updates till *I* tell you to. I want to make sure I have everything in order before I summon him here. In the meantime, I will see to it that you have all the nuts and fruit you can dream of. You deserve something for committing to fifty years of service."

"Could be seventy years of service," Iago said with what sounded like a groan. "My grandfather lived to seventy-two."

Nasir walked over to a small chest sitting on a dresser and unlocked it, producing an outrageously large red jewel. Iago's eyes widened.

"What's that you've got right there?"

"Oh, just something I took from the Sultan's treasure room when he wasn't looking. That man is maddeningly foolish. Leaving his treasures out for his grand vizier to pluck, leaving his daughter one less jewel." Nasir and Iago both laughed. Nasir placed the jewel on the bottom of Iago's cage. "You can have this if you want . . . maybe when you return to Jafar, you can use it to take an early retirement. I'll even second the motion."

Iago snatched the jewel in his claw and placed it under a bed of straw in his cage. "I guess working with you while we're in town wouldn't be that bad. Speaking of which, let's get that searching spell going and find the kid and the charm already. There are riches to be had."

"With pleasure." Nasir remembered the child's face clearly in his mind. He had black hair and big brown eyes. Daa would certainly know who this child was, and Nasir was willing to do whatever it took to find out more. He'd come this far. He wasn't stopping now.

SEVENTEEN

MUKHTARISM NUMBER 2:
NO HOLE IS SO DEEP
YOU CAN'T DIG YOURSELF OUT OF IT.

Aladdin hesitated on his way up to Mukhtar's quarters. There was no way he was going to lie to Mukhtar when it was just the two of them, but he was still worried about how Mukhtar would react. It wasn't just the grand vizier that was troubling him. Mukhtar had said the Night Bazaar only let in those who were worthy. And now he and Abu had stolen something. What if it kept Mukhtar from ever being invited back?

"Come on, Al." Mukhtar started up the steps and expected him to follow.

Abu started to whine again. Fatima shot him a triumphant look as Malik just shrugged. Kalila was the only one who smiled at Aladdin encouragingly. Aladdin had no choice. He headed up the stairs.

When they'd slept in Mukhtar's quarters the other night, the room had been dark, so Aladdin hadn't gotten a good look. But now, with candles lit everywhere, he could see the room was sparsely furnished but clean. A bed was made up next to the window, and a table and two chairs sat beside it. A pot of what smelled like soup was cooking over an open fire, and a hand-carved chest sat under the window. The wood had been hand-painted yellow and it was carved with stars, much like the ornamental display above Mukhtar's shop door. Both things resembled the constellations he'd seen on the ceiling in the Night Bazaar. Aladdin looked closer. Were the stars on the chest glowing? He blinked twice, straining to see for sure, when Mukhtar stepped in front of him.

"Have a seat." Mukhtar motioned to the chairs at the table as he sat down. He was so tall, the chair looked like a child's when he sat in it. "Apple?"

Aladdin shook his head. He was too nervous to eat.

"You sure? Fatima is right about one thing. You do look green." Mukhtar took a bite of an apple. "Why don't you tell me what happened tonight."

Aladdin's stomach tightened. "It was like I told you — I gave Arif the totem and he gave me the note. That's it."

Mukhtar leaned closer. "So . . . what did you think?"

Aladdin blinked. "Think?" His heart started to beat faster again.

Mukhtar broke out with a laugh. "Of the Night Bazaar!" He raised a bushy eyebrow in Aladdin's direction. "Tell me everything! I know that look on your face — I've seen it on others the first time they visited the Night Bazaar, too. Daa can be a bit overwhelming."

Aladdin felt his whole body start to relax. "You know Daa?"

"Of course!" Mukhtar opened his arms wide. "He's the keeper of the door. He's been around for centuries, and he'd never let you in if I wasn't right — you are worthy. So what did you think? The place is both magical and mysterious, which can be nerve-racking the first time around, I know. Especially with all those entrances and exits to the tents — up, down, sideways. Sometimes it makes me dizzy." He tsked. "One time I was stuck on the ceiling for hours! But eventually you figure out tricks, and next time you go, you'll know your way around better."

Aladdin faltered. What if the potion kept Mukhtar from ever being invited back again? "Next time?"

"Of course! Tell me it didn't feel like you were always meant to visit. Like they knew you — some probably did. Did they say anything to you about . . . your journey?" Mukhtar questioned curiously. "Like, could you feel the place calling to you?"

"Yes," Aladdin said without hesitation. Maybe it had been the Night Bazaar calling him all along. He'd assumed the voice was attached to magicked items, but maybe it was the Night Bazaar beckoning him. Or the pull of Agrabah? Were they one and the same? It was clear there was magick within this city and Aladdin couldn't deny — even with all that had gone wrong that night — that it was exciting. "I've never been anywhere like that before. It made me feel special." He frowned and thought of the potion again. "But . . ."

"But what?"

Should he mention the potion? Instead, he asked something else that had been on his mind. "Why would the Night Bazaar pick me? Why would you even? You've known Kalila, Malik, and Fatima forever. Why not ask them to get the note to Arif? You heard Fatima — she didn't understand, either. And she doesn't even know you were sending me to the Night Bazaar! She just knew you trusted me with something you didn't trust her with. I'm trying to understand why."

Mukhtar's expression was serious and it was a moment before he spoke. "You have *it*, Al. I saw it the first time I met you. You're meant to be here."

Aladdin felt his heart start to drum. "In Agrabah you mean? How do you know that?"

Mukhtar stared at him, as if he could see all the way to Aladdin's soul. "I can't explain everything yet. You just have to trust me. You've got something inside you that the Night Bazaar can see even if you can't yet."

"And what's that?" Aladdin pushed, his fingers brushing against the bottle in his pocket again. He could hear the bottle whispering to him again, begging to be uncorked. He concentrated on ignoring it.

Mukhtar leaned forward, his eyes bright. "You're a Diamond in the rough."

Aladdin jumped up, panicked. "I heard that phrase tonight in the Night Bazaar. And people keep talking about diamonds. *You've* talked about them, too. Why'd you call me a diamond? What *is* a diamond?"

Mukhtar smiled. "It means you're special. On the outside you may think you look ordinary, but where it counts . . . in here . . ." He pointed to his own chest. "You are extraordinary. You are worthy. You know how to do what's right."

Mukhtar was giving him too much credit. He'd taken a bottle from the Night Bazaar. Well, it was Abu who took it, but still. What would Mukhtar say if he knew? What about the grand vizier's potion? Did he tell Mukhtar what could happen if it were miscast? Look what someone had done to Mukhtar's shop when they didn't know Aladdin was here. If the grand vizier found him or the others . . . he closed his eyes in worry. He didn't know what to do.

Mukhtar shook his head. "Listen, Al. I know you've been through a lot the last few days, but it's all going to work out the way it should. Just remember your Mukhtarisms and be smart out there. Be careful who you trust. And above all else, protect that charm around your neck."

Aladdin opened his eyes and his hand went to his neck. "My necklace? Why do I need to protect that?" Did Mukhtar know it glowed? Could he know the grand vizier had a charm, too, one that glowed as well? Were they connected somehow? He wanted to ask so many things, but then he'd have to explain what happened outside the Night Bazaar with the grand vizier.

"You said your parents left it to you," Mukhtar pointed out. "Nothing is more important than family." He was quiet for a moment. "You know, my parents were taken from me when I was young, too, by the Azalam as well."

"I didn't know that," Aladdin said in surprise. "So you know how awful those bandits are."

"Yes. They're a small, power-hungry, and selfish group. I was on the streets until . . . well, I got on my feet with help from some good people. People from Agrabah who are nothing like the Azalam." He looked into the fireplace and stared at the flames. "These people taught me all I know. I don't know if I can ever repay them for what they gave me. In some ways I thought I failed them, too . . . but now. Maybe I still have a chance. I won't let the Azalam succeed. That much power in the wrong hands could be catastrophic."

"So the Azalam are in Agrabah right now?" Aladdin asked worriedly. The way the grand vizier was talking, Aladdin was almost positive he was one of them. Should he tell Mukhtar? But the encounter with the necklace . . . he didn't want to tell him about the necklace.

Mukhtar's smile was grim. "I believe so, but don't you worry." He stood and clapped Aladdin on his back. "I'm going to make them think Agrabah is the most boring city in the world and they'll shove off again."

Aladdin couldn't think straight. Why would the grand vizier want to pay any price to have his charm? The beetle charm was broken, making it less valuable. Was the grand vizier's charm broken, too? Were they two halves of one whole? What would happen if the two halves became one? The idea made Aladdin even more anxious.

"Are you sure you're not hungry?" Mukhtar took a second apple and bit into it, too. Aladdin shook his head. "Suit yourself," Mukhtar said. "Now let's see what Arif has to say."

Mukhtar pulled the message out of his pocket. The paper was sheer, allowing Aladdin to see a faint outline of black lettering on the other side. Mukhtar read it and sighed.

"Unfortunately, it's exactly as I suspected." Mukhtar tore up the message and dunked it in a cup of water. The paper disintegrated immediately, a hazy yellow mist appearing where it had once been. "There's a storm brewing, Al." He stared at his fireplace as if willing it to give him answers. "And I think it's going to be a mean one." He looked up. "I need to prepare and you should go get some sleep. Tell the others we'll clean up the rest of the shop in the morning."

Aladdin did as he was told, but he kept looking back at Mukhtar. How could Arif know anything about a storm? Aladdin sensed Mukhtar wouldn't explain himself. He was so cryptic. All Aladdin knew was the prickling sensation at the back of his neck had returned. He hesitated at the top of the steps. Was he wrong not to tell Mukhtar about the future-telling potion bottle and grand vizier? Or did Mukhtar already have enough to worry about as it was?

Tell Mukhtar, said the voice in his head, but he still couldn't find the words. His lips were dry. His knees started to shake.

"Al?"

Aladdin looked back at Mukhtar, who was staring at him.

"You sure you're okay, kid?"

"Yeah. Just tired. Falling through the sky will do that to you," Aladdin joked.

Mukhtar actually laughed. "Should have warned you about the stars." He stared at the chest in the corner of the room. "There is nothing like them." He looked back at Aladdin. "I'll let you go then . . . but are you sure there is nothing else that happened tonight that you want to share?"

This was his chance to spill everything. He could feel the bottle burning a hole in his pocket, whispering to him again to be opened, but he pushed the thought aside. Mukhtar already knew the Azalam were in Agrabah. He probably knew about the grand vizier, too. Aladdin would just have to investigate the Azalam on his own and keep his new friends safe. In a short amount of time, he'd felt more settled with Abu, Kalila, Malik. and even Fatima than he ever had with the caravan. He wouldn't let anything happen to them. Aladdin smiled. "Nope. Nothing at all. Good night, Mukhtar."

Mukhtar raised a hand in farewell. "Good night, Al."

EIGHTEEN

NASIR

Nasir did not enjoy glistening.

But unfortunately, running through the streets of Agrabah on a humid evening meant he arrived back at the palace both sweaty and out of breath. Two things he detested.

But the bath he intended to have his servants fix for him was worth it.

He had gotten exactly what he needed at the Night Bazaar, which thankfully revealed itself to him again the minute he drew near, thanks to some clever spells on his part that made him appear worthy. Whether his intentions were actually good or evil, his spells saw to it that the Night Bazaar didn't know. All the place knew was that he was worthy. He'd made Daa see that personally.

Nasir closed his chamber doors with a loud clap, waking the macaw who was sleeping on a windowsill. The bird jumped.

"Did you get it? What happened? What took you too long?"

"Patience, Iago," Nasir purred, smoothing his thawb, as he approached the bird. "I know exactly who that dreadful child is."

"And? Don't hold me in suspense! Who is the kid?"

Nasir smiled slyly and laced his fingers together, unable to ignore the excitement at knowing that he was one step closer. "Not only do I know who he is, but I know where he is."

"Where is he?"

"The boy's name is Aladdin, and he works here in the city at something called Mukhtar's 'Junk' Shop." Nasir shuddered at the word *junk*.

"Junk? Wow, it's worse than we thought. Why would this kid have the charm?"

"Well, that's where things get interesting." Nasir unfolded a small scrap of paper with tiny, neat handwriting on it. "After some negotiations, I got Daa to tell me who Aladdin was meeting with in the Night Bazaar — a traitor of the Azalam who knew more than just where I could find the boy. He gave Aladdin a message for someone, a message that changes everything. I made this traitor give me the same message."

"And?" Iago flew over to Nasir's shoulder to look down at the paper. "What's with you dragging this out?"

"It said, 'The Azalam are in the city and grow closer to their goal.'"

"That's true. We are close."

"Yes, but this is the interesting part of the message. It also said: 'They have half the charm, but still do not know of the Diamond in the rough in their midst they need to open the Cave.'"

"Diamond? What's a diamond?"

"I thought they were referring to a jewel when I first read it, but now I'm not so sure," Nasir said, tapping his chin. "Why would we need both halves of the charm *and* another jewel? No, the diamond must be a metaphor for something else. This diamond, so to speak, is needed to open the Cave along with the charm."

"A spell maybe?"

"No, then they'd just use the word 'spell,'" Nasir assumed, growing frustrated. "What else could 'diamond' refer to?"

"You said diamond in the rough, right? If it's not a jewel, and it's here in the city, and it's not the cave, could it be . . . a person?"

Nasir's eyes widened. "Yessss. The Diamond in the rough. One who doesn't know they're worthy of opening the cave."

"Someone like a street rat?"

This was making more sense by the moment. "It might be, Iago. Think about it!" Nasir grew excited as he began to piece the clues together. "This could be why our ancestors were so unsuccessful when they tried to open the Cave on their own. We might have had the whole charm, but without this 'Diamond in the rough,' the Cave couldn't be opened!" He cried out: "I can't believe we never thought of this before!" He'd cracked information no one in the Azalam had before.

"Yowza! Wait till Jafar gets a load of this news."

Nasir whipped his head around to look at the bird. His heart practically stopped at the thought of his brother learning the truth and showing up here before the job was done. "Remember our deal, Iago. No updates for my brother till we know exactly what we're dealing with." Nasir thought some more. "We still don't know how this Aladdin came to possess the charm."

"Maybe the kid stole it."

"Likely, and yet . . ." Nasir knew there was something he was still missing here. But what? "With the right pressure, and a foreboding presence such as myself, why wouldn't the little thief be willing to accept a reward for handing it over to me? I offered him anything his heart desired and he refused. No, he must think the charm is rightfully his." Nasir's expression darkened. "Which it is not."

"So what are you saying: Do you think this kid is the actual Diamond in the rough? Feels like a stretch. And who ever heard of a Cave opening for only one person? It's just a cave."

"I know, Iago, but if the Cave can only be opened with both halves of the charm, wouldn't it stand to reason that the person with the charm had to be special, too?" Nasir wondered. "Aladdin has the charm, but he was clearly bringing the note to someone. The question is who. Are they the Diamond? Or is it this street rat?"

"So? Let's go get the kid and make him talk!"

Nasir snapped his fingers. "Good idea, Iago. Let's smoke them out and see where this Mukhtar's shop is. I'm sure that's where the street rat is hiding."

Nasir dropped the location spell into the cauldron and said an incantation, and suddenly the potion began to swirl, clouding up like they were in a sandstorm and then clearing. That's when Nasir found himself staring at the door to the shop. The ornamental display over the door had a very familiar cloud of stars etched into it. "Yes, of course," he purred.

"What?"

"This Mukhtar actually runs a charm shop, is a fan of the Night Bazaar, and he's employing the street rat." He turned to Iago. "If Aladdin was bringing him the note, then I bet Mukhtar knows what that charm is worth! And if he doesn't, then I can easily force him to hand over Aladdin and the charm. If he's this Diamond the note speaks of, and he has the charm, then we have all we need to finally open the Cave."

"Now you're thinking! So? What are we waiting for?"

Nasir's heart was beating fast. Victory was within reach. "Faaris!" Nasir roared. "Faaris!"

The door to his private chambers flew open and a bleary-eyed

Faaris stood in his night garments. "Sir? Is everything all right? I'm sorry I don't have any new information yet. I'm trying."

"I have news, Faaris." Nasir folded his long fingers together, much like he saw his older brother do when he was hatching a plan. He looked at Iago. "No thanks to you, I now know exactly where to find the boy with the charm I seek."

"You do?" Faaris looked relieved. "Should I get dressed and go fetch him?"

"Actually, no," Nasir surprised himself by saying. "Let's wait."

"Squawk!"

Nasir ignored Iago. "There's no need to cause a scene in the middle of the night and wake the whole city. I'm thinking it's best to do this when others are preoccupied. Let's fetch this Aladdin and his friend Mukhtar during the new-moon dinner. I'll tell you where and when to bring them to me."

"Yes, sir," Faaris said, and backed out of the room.

"You think that's a good idea?" Iago asked. "The kid knows who you are — what if he tells his boss about you and the guy tries to escape before the new moon? It's still three days away!"

"The man has a business here, Iago — a pathetic one, but still. He couldn't afford to close his shop and run before the new-moon dinner. And Aladdin? He's a street rat. He has nowhere to turn. No friends to rely on. No, we must prepare before we strike. We have no idea what a Diamond in the rough is capable of. In the morning I will have Faaris send some guards to survey the shop and make sure this Mukhtar doesn't flee. We will learn more about this Diamond business and grab Mukhtar right before the new moon when he least expects it."

"All right. If you're sure. You don't want to screw this up — this isn't like that time in Timeron. You fail again and the Azalam will finish you."

He hated thinking about Timeron. He'd been rash. Younger with more youthful skin. (Oh, how he loved his youthful skin! Hopefully the tonics he was using would bring it back.) He was smarter now. He wanted power greater than any his brother could achieve. He wanted his own kingdom. He wouldn't do anything to mess that up. "I know what I'm doing. Don't you worry. By nightfall of the next new moon, entry to the Cave of Wonders will be ours."

"You're sure?"

"Yes," Nasir snapped. He would not tolerate being questioned by a bird. "And to be certain, perhaps we will get our hands on that future-casting potion Aladdin stole and see it all for ourselves."

"Isn't that the one you said if it was done wrong, it could destroy everything around us? I want to get out of this overcrowded dust bowl as much as you do, but I don't want to be a cooked bird to do it."

"I know what I'm doing, Iago." Nasir was a powerful sorcerer. He wouldn't fear a potion, even one as tricky as this. He walked to the balcony and looked out at the vast city below, trying to picture what Aladdin was doing at that exact moment.

It didn't really matter, did it? In a few days' time, the street rat's life and all the Cave had to offer would be his.

NINETEEN

MUKHTARISM NUMBER 54:
IF YOU FIND YOURSELF IN HOT WATER,
ASK YOUR FRIENDS TO PULL YOU OUT.

The Sultan loved any excuse for a celebration. In his mind, who didn't welcome a chance to sing, dance, have new food, and meet up with old friends? The birth of a baby elephant, the time the Sultan discovered a new favorite spice, a new-moon dinner. The Sultan made sure that the community came togther for a meal at least once a month, gathering late in the afternoon and celebrating till deep into the night.

To prepare, people were at the marketplace early that weekend morning, picking up ingredients or buying new jewelry to wear or even a thawb or two as tents rose in the background of the palace for the meal. Those who had passed the palace gates said stages were being built, dancers were practicing numbers, and lanterns were lined up to light the path to the dinner.

Everyone couldn't help but note that this dinner seemed bigger than new-moon dinners that had come before. Could it be that their new grand vizier had a hand in the merriment? Whatever the reason, people were excited. This new-moon dinner was poised to be the largest event Agrabah had ever seen and would remain so for quite some time. (Sure, a royal wedding would be an even bigger deal, but Princess Jasmine was only ten. She had some time.)

Aladdin, for one, had never seen anything like this level of excitement. He'd never been to a dinner at a palace before, either. But instead of anticipation, all he felt was dread. The grand vizier and how badly he had wanted Aladdin's beetle charm was all he could think about. He knew he should have told Mukhtar when he'd had the chance. The grand vizier was clearly dangerous, which is why it made him anxious that it had been two whole days and the grand vizier still hadn't come searching for him.

"Aladdin?" Kalila touched his arm, pulling him from his dark thoughts. "You ready?"

The shop had been cleaned and put back together; new vases, jewels, and mirrors arriving out of storage to replace what had been destroyed. Aladdin wasn't sure where the stuff had even come from — Mukhtar hadn't let them out to work for three days after the shop was ransacked. But tonight was the big dinner for the new moon and even Mukhtar knew it was time to get back to work.

"People are going to be so excited about the dinner at the palace, they're going to be distracted," he had told them that morning during breakfast. "This is the perfect time to rescue some magick items that are in the wrong hands. Save them and bring them to me!"

Fatima gave him a look. "You mean look for the fancy things and take them when no one is looking, right?"

Mukhtar smiled. "Exactly!"

Abu started to whine. *What about the stolen potion?* he seemed to be trying to remind him. How could Aladdin forget? It wasn't bad enough that the grand vizier had seen his charm and wanted it, what if he tracked them down and got his hand on the future-casting potion

Abu had stolen? Even if he didn't find them, what if he was using the potion he bought at the Night Bazaar and accidentally destroyed Agrabah? Aladdin glanced over at Mukhtar polishing a vase and wished again he had the guts to tell his boss what had happened that night. He didn't want Mukhtar or the others getting in trouble for something he or Abu had done or had failed to do!

Aladdin hadn't felt this alone since the day he lost Elham in the market. Every time he thought of the Bedouin and his failure to find them in the city, or heard of anyone searching for him, his heart felt a little heavier. More than anything, he wished he could find Elham and tell her how sorry he was for getting lost that day.

But if he found the Bedouin, what would he do then? Would he go back with them, or would he stay here? He couldn't deny how he felt about Agrabah even if he'd somehow found himself in a murky situation at the moment. Was he making things worse for his new friends by being here? Or would this storm pass, too? Mukhtar said protecting his necklace was important, and Aladdin had managed to do that so far, so he was still doing something right. *Everything will be fine*, he told himself.

"What's the plan for this afternoon?" Aladdin asked. "How are we distracting people while we do our job?"

"Old lady in the way," Kalila told the group, grabbing a thawb from a basket and throwing him one. She took a piece of wood from a pile near the door and used it as a cane, and walked slowly in front of the group. "Excuse me, dearie! Don't mind me," she croaked. "I move slow."

"Excuse me! I'm trying to get my cart through the crowd," Malik complained, acting like a shopkeeper.

Fatima jumped out in front of Kalila. "Give her a moment! You're going to run this poor woman over!" she said as if they had rehearsed it a thousand times before.

This was Aladdin's sign.

"I'll help you, old woman!" he said, swooping in to give Kalila his arm as she reached from under her robe and grabbed a small silver bell sitting on a nearby table. She reached into her robe and placed the bell in a satchel she carried. That satchel would be passed over to Fatima, then to Malik, then guarded by Abu. The goal was to keep the items moving in case anyone was being watched.

Next Aladdin did something that wasn't part of the plan: He hugged Malik. "Thanks, big guy!" he said, holding him tight even as Malik tried to shrug him off. "Sorry to get in the way of your cart."

"Ugh! Let go!" Malik tried to pry Aladdin off, but he held on, watching Kalila slink away out of the corner of his eye.

Aladdin had a strong grip. It came in handy sometimes.

The mock run-through over, the group burst out laughing.

"What was the hug for?" Malik asked Aladdin.

"I felt like it gave Kalila extra time to get away," Aladdin said with a shrug.

Mukhtar applauded. "Nice moves, *team*," he said with a wink. "Make me proud this afternoon."

"You really aren't coming to the dinner later?" Kalila asked. "It sounds like it's going to be so much fun."

"Battling poets, a menagerie of animals, even an elephant parade!" Malik reminded him.

Fatima fanned her nose. "I hope they clean up after the elephants better than they did last time."

"I am sure it will be another great dinner thrown by the Sultan," Mukhtar said with a smile, and Aladdin noticed him staring his way, "but I have work of my own to do." He pointed to Aladdin. "You lot stay together, you hear me? On a day like today, it's not a good idea to wander off."

"You afraid we're going to get lost?" Fatima said with a laugh.

"I mean it, stick together and all of you be back here by sundown," Mukhtar said, sounding fatherlike.

They all groaned.

"But the real party doesn't start till then! I think the battling poets start after sundown!" Kalila complained.

"Sundown," Mukhtar insisted. "Nothing good happens after dark." There was more grumbling. "If it's that great, we will all go back out together, but be here at sundown."

"Okay," they all agreed, heading out the door.

"Al?" Mukhtar called, and Aladdin looked at his boss, who seemed nervous. "Be careful out there today and remember what I said — always be on watch and keep your charm close."

Keep your charm close, Aladdin repeated internally, annoyed at himself for not realizing this before.

The charm was more than just a charm, wasn't it?

If he hadn't had a hunch before, he couldn't deny that he had one now. Mukhtar didn't just care about the charm because it was Aladdin's only memento of his family. There had to be something almost magicked about the rusty beetle. Why else would the grand vizier have been so anxious to get his hands on it?

It was clear: Their charms were connected — but what would happen if the pieces were reunited? Aladdin wasn't sure, but he did know Mukhtar obviously didn't want that reunion to happen. He hesitated, desperate to ask Mukhtar about it, but he couldn't do so in front of the others. His heart beat faster. "I'll protect it with my life," he promised.

"Your life?" Malik laughed.

Mukhtar swallowed hard. "Ah, Al, don't be dramatic. I just don't want you to lose your only possession."

Abu hopped on Aladdin's back as he grabbed a satchel from the basket near the door. Kalila got her beard and robe, and Fatima and Malik grabbed the instruments. Everyone was talking at once about what they wanted to see first (some singing-bird routine that was a favorite of the Sultan's) and what they hoped to eat (kdaameh, because who didn't like roasted sugared chickpeas?). It was only when Aladdin was out the door and the others had walked a bit ahead that he turned to look at Abu.

"You have it on you?" Aladdin asked.

Abu lifted his fez, and Aladdin saw the yellow bottle nestled against the monkey's head.

"Good. We get rid of that potion today. Safely. If we can figure out how."

Abu squeaked.

"I know. I'm not sure how to destroy it, either, without it falling into the wrong hands, but we can't keep it at Mukhtar's. What if the shop is raided? Or the grand vizier finds me?" Aladdin glanced around the street as if expecting an answer to appear. "We need to get rid of it before either of those things happen."

Abu whined.

"I know you didn't mean it, buddy. We just have to clean up our mess. Get rid of that potion and make sure it doesn't wind up with the grand vizier. *And* make sure that the grand vizier doesn't find us and try to take my necklace again." He looked over his shoulder. "We have to be extra careful and hope he doesn't recognize us today."

There were more squeaks from Abu.

"I know it's going to be dark soon," Aladdin said. "So we have a lot to do — get rid of the bottle, avoid the grand vizier, and make sure he doesn't find out where we live or come after Mukhtar or our friends."

"Who are you talking to?"

Aladdin froze. Fatima was standing in an alleyway, covered in shadows, behind a giant barrel, almost entirely unseen.

Aladdin's heart beat fast. "Hey, Fatima."

She stepped out. The others were still walking ahead of them. "Were you talking to your monkey?"

Abu and Aladdin looked at each other. "Well, yeah. We get each other." Abu leaned in closer and grunted. "We've got our own language."

Fatima shook her head. "Weird." She paused and looked down at the ground, her sandals scuffing the dirt. "So I wanted to apologize for . . . you know . . . for the other day. I shouldn't have blamed you for the break-in."

"Oh." Aladdin wasn't expecting an apology. Not from Fatima. And for all they knew, the break-in *was* his fault. Bumping into the grand vizier, stealing the potion — other stressful things were very much his fault. "It's fine."

"It's not." Fatima looked up at him, her green eyes watery. "I get really protective of what I love. Mukhtar and the others are my family. I lost my parents when I was little, like Mukhtar did. He took me in. I feel like I have to look out for him and Malik and Kalila, too. I don't want anything to happen to them or to what we've built at the charm shop. We've worked so hard."

Aladdin understood what Fatima meant. This was her family, and in a way, they were becoming his, too. That's why he had to protect them. "I think I know what you mean," he said, and Abu whined in agreement.

Fatima nodded. "Good. I just wanted to explain why I've been so hard on you. Mukhtar hasn't taken anyone in since Malik two years ago. If you want to be part of our team, then great. But if you're just passing through, we don't need the trouble," Fatima said, her voice stronger. "We've all lost enough as it is, and Mukhtar has been acting so weird since you came around."

"He has?" Aladdin bit the inside of his cheek.

"Telling you to protect that dirty charm around your neck. It's just strange. It makes me think you're both keeping secrets." She stared him down, as if waiting for him to say otherwise.

Fatima was intimidating. "Me? A secret? Never! Right, Abu?" Abu screeched. "See? No secrets. I just want a roof over my head and to make Mukhtar proud." *And get rid of this bottle and make sure the grand vizier doesn't know how to find me or do anything to the rest of you.*

Fatima nodded. "Okay, then we have nothing to worry about, I guess."

"Guys! Come on!" Malik called up ahead. "The parade is starting."

Fatima ran ahead and Aladdin followed at a slower pace. The sun was high in the sky and the streets ahead were crowded with people who could be carrying magicked items and shiny stuff that would help keep Mukhtar's Magick Shop open another day. The team had a job to do. Aladdin just hoped he could concentrate and pull it off.

"Ready, Abu?" The monkey grunted in agreement. "Let's keep our heads down and get to work."

The next few hours were a blur, and Aladdin was so busy he couldn't think of a single place to dump a dangerous potion. Instead he stayed on the lookout for the grand vizier, did "old lady in the way" several times, and hunted for magicked things. Malik found a bell, Fatima felt called to a crystal headband, and Kalila grabbed a small monkey statue that looked a bit like Abu. Aladdin, however, came up empty. Despite his pep talk to himself, he couldn't focus. His eyes were constantly on the growing crowd, searching for the grand vizier. Between the battling poets and vendors selling new-moon snacks, the crowd grew so large that he eventually lost sight of Kalila, then Malik, then Fatima. Only Abu stuck by his side.

"Uh-oh! Uh-oh!" said Abu as the crowd thickened to the point where it was hard to move.

"It's okay, buddy," Aladdin said, craning his neck to look for the others as he got jostled from the front and behind. There were too many eyes around to get rid of the potion now, but the good news was he still hadn't seen the grand vizier. He'd just have to go home with the potion and hope Mukhtar kept his promise that they could all go to the dinner together later on.

Aladdin . . .

Aladdin froze. The voice was back. Was it the Night Bazaar? Something magicked? Or was it just a voice in his head?

Careful, Aladdin! Focus!

He whirled around, the sound of laughter, an oud, and someone singing intensifying. Was this his imagination? The wind?

Aladdin . . . help!

Help? Aladdin's hand instinctively went to his neck. This voice was different. Something was wrong.

Help, Aladdin!

That voice sounded like Kalila!

Abu started to whine, and he tightened his grip around Aladdin's neck as if he sensed the voice, too. Aladdin spun around, searching for his friends in vain when he suddenly saw mist moving toward him. No one else seemed to notice it.

Aladdin held his breath, half expecting to see the Night Bazaar's tent and stars appear beneath his feet and above his head. Instead, the crowd began to quiet as if the world was falling away. Aladdin looked down at the mist at his feet and noticed something unusual —

this smoke was the color of ash, as if it was brought on by fire. It felt different. *Very* different.

And then the charm around his neck began to warm.

The grand vizier, he thought.

Help, Aladdin! Run!

This wasn't the Night Bazaar calling him. Something told Aladdin his friends were in trouble.

"Hang on, Abu!" he cried, racing down the streets away from the mist, going the only route he knew. (Which meant he was ignoring Mukhtarism nineteen: Never go home when you're being followed.) Aladdin no longer had a choice. If Kalila, Malik, and Fatima were in trouble, he had to act fast. He'd confess to Mukhtar about what happened with the grand vizier and about the stolen potion. Maybe Mukhtar would be upset, but he would help him. Of that, Aladdin was now certain. He couldn't do it alone.

Aladdin kept running, looking back as the mist rolled closer and closer, reminding him of the sandstorm from that first day in Agrabah. Abu shrieked and clung tighter to Aladdin's neck.

"We're fine, Abu!" Aladdin lied because the truth was he wasn't sure he was going to be able to outrun this thing. But then, finally, Mukhtar's door appeared and Aladdin burst through it, slamming it behind him. He was breathing so hard it took a moment to catch his breath.

That's when he realized the place was dark.

"Mukhtar?" Aladdin called out. It was after sundown. Wasn't that when they were all supposed to be back? "Kalila? Fatima? Malik?"

There was no answer.

Aladdin lit a lamp and rushed to the stairs, heading up to Mukhtar's quarters. "Mukhtar?"

Mukhtar wasn't there, either.

Aladdin's heart began to beat faster. Mukhtar was supposed to be there. His friends, too. Aladdin bit the inside of his cheek and thought back: When was the last time he'd actually seen any of them in the crowd? Had it been hours ago? His charm warmed his chest, but he tried to ignore the sensation and get his thoughts together.

Had the grand vizier found out where he lived and taken his friends? Or was he being dramatic?

He rushed back down the stairs with Abu on his back and held the lantern out to see if anyone was waiting for him in the shadows.

No one was there, but the mist had found its way inside, making the shop feel like it was shrinking. Abu began to panic. Aladdin pulled open the doors to get some air, but that only made matters worse. The mist had thickened outside, looking like soup. The sounds of the dinner for the new moon had faded away.

Aladdin . . .

Aladdin . . . *help!*

Aladdin felt the hair on his neck stand up. His charm was almost burning a hole into his chest now. It started to glow and there was nothing Aladdin could do to hide it from onlookers.

Onlookers. Aladdin did a double take. Outside the shop, a woman with a broom was frozen mid-sweep. To his left, a child running with cymbals had stopped mid-clap. A girl with her mouth open was not moving. The rest of the world was quiet.

Something was very wrong.

"Abu?" Aladdin whispered, his body going numb. "I think Agrabah is under a spell and we're the only ones not in it."

Abu whined in agreement, placing his paws more firmly around Aladdin's neck.

"Squawk! Squawk!"

A red macaw flew past them, startling Abu as it landed on top of Mukhtar's open door.

Aladdin stared at it in wonder. How could the bird still move when the rest of Agrabah was frozen in time?

"*Squawk! Squawk!* Aladdin!"

Aladdin jumped. "Hey. Did that bird just say my name?" he asked Abu.

"*Squawk!*" the bird called again. "Better follow me, Aladdin!"

The bird knew his name! And it wanted Aladdin to follow him. Was this the grand vizier's doing? It had to be. Aladdin felt himself grow angry. "What do you want with me? Where are my friends?"

"*Squawk!* In trouble! Friends in trouble! Aladdin, follow me!"

Aladdin's pulse raced. "What do you mean in trouble? What have you done with them? Who do you work for?" The smoke seemed to wrap around them, like a rope. Abu began to panic, but Aladdin stood firm. He wasn't going to let some bird tell him what to do. "Answer me!"

"You know who has them, Aladdin! Don't be a fool!"

Aladdin *did* know even if he tried to deny it himself. It was time for him to stop what he'd started the day he failed to tell Mukhtar about what really happened at the Night Bazaar.

Aladdin looked at the bird. "Take me to the grand vizier."

TWENTY

MUKHTARISM NUMBER 49:
NEVER WORK ON AN EMPTY STOMACH.
(IF YOU CAN HELP IT!)

Aladdin followed the macaw to the edge of the city and beyond.

He hadn't been outside the city walls since the day Kalila had walked him back to the Bedouin and they weren't there. For a moment, Aladdin found himself searching for Elham once more, half expecting to find the tribe waiting for him, Elham greeting him with open arms.

Instead, all he saw were the mountains in the distance and mounds of blowing sand.

"*Squawk!* Keep up, Aladdin! Keep up!"

The bird wasn't slowing down. Wherever the grand vizier had taken Aladdin's friends, it wasn't within the city walls. Did the grand vizier have Mukhtar, too? There was something about Mukhtar that made Aladdin think the guy wouldn't have gone quietly, but if he'd gotten away, where was he now? He wouldn't have just left Aladdin and the others to fend for themselves . . . would he?

Aladdin kept moving, walking through the darkened desert until he thought he could walk no more. He was alone. Impossibly alone. It was something he was growing tired of. It's how he felt with the Bedouin when Elham wasn't by his side and it was how he felt now, without Mukhtar and the others or Agrabah there to guide him.

That's when the bird perched itself on a lone horse that appeared in the darkness.

"Uh-oh," said Abu.

Uh-oh was right. Where had the horse come from? It hadn't been there a minute ago. Aladdin refused to let the bird see he was anxious. "Nothing to be worried about here, Abu. Last I checked, the grand vizier wasn't a horse." Abu started to laugh and Aladdin felt his stomach unclench. Humor might help him through this. "Besides, a horse means we won't have to walk anymore."

Have faith, Aladdin.

Aladdin stopped laughing and listened to the whisper on the wind. Was that the voice again? The night sky was cloudless and filled with stars, but a soft wind had brought in more whispers. He wasn't sure if they came from the stolen potion he still had on his person, or from the voice itself, but suddenly Aladdin didn't feel so afraid.

He wasn't alone.

He had Abu. He had these whispers that made him stronger. And he had his charm, which Mukhtar had said he should protect at all costs. The farther they had walked, the brighter his charm glowed. He could feel the heat on his chest. *Have faith.*

He did. Whatever he was about to face, he could do it with the charm around his neck, the one thing his parents had left him with. He wasn't alone. He had to remember that.

"*Squawk!* Get on the horse, birdbrain, or you can say goodbye to your little friends!"

"Wow, Abu, maybe we should get you speaking classes with this bird. He's cranky, but he's got the evil bird dialogue down," Aladdin said, and Abu snickered.

The bird seemed to roll his eyes. "*Squawk!* I mean it! On the horse! Now!"

"Where are we headed?" Aladdin tried to stall so he could think this through. What if this horse was leading him to his death so the grand vizier could take his charm? He imagined riding right off the edge of a cliff.

Then again, would the bird want to kill him before the grand vizier got what he wanted?

"*Squawk!* You're wasting time. Your friends don't have much left."

Abu started to whine again. It felt like he was saying, *This isn't a good idea.*

Go, Aladdin . . . it's all right.

For the first time, Aladdin realized the voice inside his head that he'd been hearing sounded female. It was warm like the sun and the beetle burning his neck. Maybe it was foolish, but he tried to think of this voice as his mother's, guiding him. He touched his chest, pressing his fingers to the beetle charm, and thought of his parents' last gift once more. Maybe this necklace was a good-luck charm. He had to believe that in order to have the courage to move forward now. "Fine, let's go."

Aladdin climbed on the horse and it took off as if by magic, racing across the sand that kicked up all around them. They moved so fast, Aladdin holding on to the reins with one hand and Abu with the other. The wind stung his eyes, but he forced them open, foolishly thinking he could track their path even though all that surrounded him in the desert was sand and stars. When he blinked hard, he actually thought he saw the path the horse was following glow. It wasn't a blanket of stars like the Night Bazaar had, but it was clearly a map that led them deeper and deeper into the desert.

When Aladdin looked back, the lights of Agrabah had disappeared completely, and for a moment, he felt his resolve waffle. How would he ever find his way back? The darkness felt like it would swallow them whole, but then the horse crested another ridge and a shadow appeared in the darkness: It was the grand vizier. Abu started to screech.

"Aladdin, how nice to see you again!" Nasir said, stepping closer. The charm around his own neck glowed eerily bright in the darkness, almost looking like a star. Aladdin's charm suddenly started pulsing, whispering to him.

"I'm glad you could join me to celebrate the new moon."

Aladdin climbed off the horse as Abu clung to his back. He could feel his heart race faster, but he tried to control his voice. He was not alone. "Kind of feels like we're a little far from the dinner to be part of the party, don't you think? There's nothing here."

Nasir's eyes widened. "Oh, that's where you're wrong, my little friend! I've brought entertainment!"

He pulled out a purple potion bottle and uncorked it, a familiar mist rising into the air that swirled faster and faster before a group of three kids appeared, roped together, back-to-back, their mouths gagged. It was Fatima, Malik, and Kalila. With a flick of Nasir's wrist, their gags disappeared.

"Aladdin! Help us!" his friends cried.

"Hang on!" Aladdin ran for his friends.

He barely made it a few feet before he felt a force yank him backward. He tumbled, flipping, Abu flying off his back.

"Abu!" Aladdin cried, crawling through the sand to get to his friend, who was lying facedown in the sand. *Please be okay, Abu*, he thought. He heard a tiny squeak and exhaled when he saw the tiny monkey's chest rise and fall. "Oh, thank the stars," he whispered. "Stay down."

The monkey turned his head ever so slightly and winked. Aladdin noticed Abu move his paw to the fez that had fallen off his head. The potion! He still had it.

"Abu, you clever monkey." Aladdin took the bottle and slipped it into his sleeve before Nasir could see. Maybe this future-casting potion could help them somehow.

Aladdin turned back to Nasir. "What have you done to my friend? He isn't moving!" he lied.

"Are we really that broken up about a monkey, for goodness' sake?" Nasir's high-pitched laugh carried on the wind.

Aladdin couldn't take Nasir's callousness. Even if he was faking things as a distraction, he still felt his anger bubble over. "What do you want from me?"

"Oh, Aladdin, you silly little street rat," Nasir said, laughing harder as the bird perched on his shoulder. "Don't you know by now? You have something I need and you know exactly what it is."

"*Squawk!* Riffraff!"

"I prefer to call him a street rat, Iago, because only a street rat would be foolish enough to run from a sorcerer like me."

"*Squawk!* Street rat!"

That bird has to go, too, Aladdin thought. *How am I getting out of this? Stall*, he told himself. "Riffraff? Street rat? I don't buy that. If you want what I have, then you better stop calling me names."

Nasir stared at him with interest. "A backbone! Intriguing. Name your terms."

Aladdin thought fast. "Give me my friends back and I'll give you what you want."

Nasir looked at Iago. "Hmm . . . What do you think, Iago?"

The bird looked at him. "*Squawk!* If it gets us out of this desert and back into the palace, I say go for it!"

Nasir put out a hand, his long fingers flicking impatiently. "Well, then. Hand it over."

The question was, what did Nasir really want?

Aladdin could hand over the potion and risk Nasir seeing the future, or he could hand over this charm, not knowing why the grand vizier wanted it. He had to make a choice.

Don't do it, Aladdin.

The voice was back.

"You're taking too long!" Nasir's whole body shook as he shouted. "Soon, I'll choose for you!"

Be strong.

What did the voice mean by that? He already was strong. He'd survived losing Elham and the Bedouin, and found his place in a new city that called to him from every street. He cared about the friends he lived with. They were why he was here right now. If his parents were alive, he hoped they'd be proud of him for putting others first.

Protect your legacy.

Protect your legacy? Hold on to the charm. That had to be what the voice meant. But if he handed over the bottle . . . was knowing the future worse? Could this potion do what the grand vizier's potion could? Could it be screwed up and destroy Agrabah? Aladdin wasn't sure. He took a deep breath, trying to control his nerves.

"Time's up!" Nasir roared. He closed his eyes and spoke in an ancient tongue Aladdin couldn't understand. The next thing he knew his whole body was being pulled forward through the sand. The potion in his pocket came flying out and landed right in Nasir's hand. Both Aladdin and the grand vizier looked surprised. Nasir grabbed him by his thawb.

"What is this? No, it can't be . . . Iago! Look! It is the future-casting potion that went missing from the Night Bazaar." He smiled wickedly at Aladdin. "You little thief."

"*Squawk!* Powerful potion!"

The wind whipped up and Aladdin heard more whispering. He heard his name, but he heard a million other words of encouragement as well. *Be strong.*

Nasir looked at the bottle from all angles. "How intriguing. I wasn't expecting this to appear! When I summoned what my heart desired, it brought me you and this potion." He scratched his chin. "It makes me wonder — is the potion a happy accident? Is the true thing I desire actually you, a lowly street rat, or the potion? Hmm . . ." He glanced at Aladdin with interest. "There are limits to magic, you know. Certain things cannot be stolen, they must be given, and clearly that is the case here — you were brought right to me." He glanced down at Aladdin's necklace. "Maybe you're not a street rat after all," he whispered. "Maybe you're a Diamond."

Aladdin froze. "You have your potion! Now let my friends go!"

"There was a time when I thought this potion was the most valuable thing in the world — it could show me the future. It could lead me to the charm, but I found that on my own when I met you in the Night Bazaar." His smile was sinister. "Suddenly the thing I desired most was in reach, or so I thought. All I needed was that charm!" His eyes flashed. "But it turned out I needed more than the charm. I needed you — a Diamond."

Aladdin's heart thudded in his chest. The grand vizier wanted the charm. "What is this Diamond everyone keeps talking about? Is it my charm? This dirty piece of junk? You have the potion. You wanted it that night in the Night Bazaar! I heard you talking. Take it. Just let my friends go!"

Nasir ignored him as he examined the bottle again. "True. And I certainly wouldn't want to risk wasting such a powerful potion when I already have what I desire." He winked at Aladdin and placed the potion in his pocket. "But I've always been a fan of awe and adoration. It's why I always make sure my thawb is the nicest at any party. One likes to be seen and admired, you know. And if you're not going to hand over the charm willingly — which I'm foretold must be the case — then I'll find a way to make you." He produced a white bottle from his pocket.

"What is that?" Aladdin asked worriedly.

Nasir ignored him. Instead, he whispered a few words and uncapped the white bottle. Vapors from within it oozed out, heading straight toward Aladdin's friends.

"NO!" Aladdin cried out as tiny crystals began to swirl around Fatima, Malik, and Kalila, creating a cyclone that rose higher and higher till his friends were no longer visible. Aladdin's heart constricted, fearful his friends were about to be whisked away. Instead, the sand slowly brightened, turning yellow.

Then he saw a large tail.

The sand transformed into an unearthly large scorpion whose stinger was so large, it could touch the sky. The scorpion's eight legs towered over Aladdin's friends, trapping them underneath its body like a dungeon would.

"A deathstalker," Aladdin whispered. They were one of the most dangerous scorpions in the desert. From the time he was a small boy, Elham had taught him how to watch for them in their camp. And here was one conjured like magic to be taller than the Sultan's palace.

His friends started to scream. Tears streamed down Kalila's cheeks as Malik's eyes locked on Aladdin's. "Help us!"

Aladdin turned to Nasir. "Please! Don't hurt them. I'll give you anything you want! Just call off the deathstalker!"

Nasir's eyes widened. "Anything?"

The scorpion's stinger swung precariously through the air. Another step and they'd be crushed.

"Anything!" Aladdin swore. "Please!"

Nasir smiled and the scorpion seemed to freeze, his friends still trapped beneath it. Nasir's fingers uncurled. "Hand over your necklace."

TWENTY-ONE

MUKHTARISM NUMBER 65:
DON'T GET A BIG HEAD.
(IT MAKES IT HARDER TO GET THROUGH THE SHOP DOOR.)

Aladdin's hand went to his throat. The charm felt hotter than it ever had before. The whispers intensified. The wind picked up.

It seemed silly, but Aladdin felt like his charm *wanted* to be connected with the one around Nasir's neck.

Be strong, the voice told Aladdin. *Show no fear*.

Aladdin knew the voice in his head was right, but he was still frightened. At the end of the day, he was a kid who'd come from nothing and suddenly he had something of value. He had to find a way to use it to his advantage. "Why do you want this old charm of mine?"

Nasir threw back his head and laughed. "Oh boy, don't you know by now what you have in your possession? That necklace gives you infinite power!"

"*Squawk!* Infinite power!" Iago agreed.

Aladdin stalled. "This old thing has power?"

"Yes!" Nasir said, his eyes glowing as red as Aladdin's necklace. His gaze had locked on the charm and he couldn't tear himself away.

"We've searched for the other half of this beetle for a century." He held up his own charm and Aladdin looked at it closely for the first time. The grand vizier's half of the beetle was in much better condition than his. "What I don't know is how you came in possession of such riches. Did you steal it?"

"No!" Aladdin scoffed. "It was a gift from my parents." The voices in his head grew louder, the charm's whispers almost overpowering his own thoughts.

It's your job to protect the Cave, Aladdin.

Aladdin closed his eyes, trying to block out the voices he didn't understand. Protect a cave? What did that mean? This had been his parents' charm. They were nomads. That's what he'd been told. Why would they own such a treasure?

Don't be swayed by the power! It isn't time. Not yet. Not now.

"He looks so confused, Iago! Should we tell him about the charm around his neck?" Nasir asked the bird.

"*Squawk!* You're going to have to kill him after this anyway. Why not?"

"Oh, Iago! Don't say such things. We said we'd let his friends go, why wouldn't we let him go as well?" The look Nasir gave Aladdin was so cold, the boy shivered. "Want to hear a story, Aladdin? It's a good one."

Aladdin thought for a moment. Mukhtar had told him to protect the charm. His parents had given him the charm. The voice wanted him to be strong. Maybe his charm was valuable if Nasir was this obsessed with it. He had two choices: If he kept the necklace, his friends would die. If he handed it over, it was clear he'd soon die, too.

He was alone in the middle of nowhere. All he had with him was a monkey playing dead and some confusing voices in his head. He had a horse at his disposal, but a single horse couldn't carry them all out of here. How was he going to save them all?

He needed time. Time to formulate a plan. Time to hold on to his charm. Time required getting Nasir to keep talking. "I like stories. Why not?"

Nasir grinned. "It starts a long time ago — centuries ago, in fact, and involves the Cave of Wonders, the likes of which this world has never seen. Oh, Aladdin, to hear them tell the tales! This cave has things you couldn't possibly dream up — things that don't exist in your boss's ridiculous little charm shop." The grand vizier and the bird laughed. "I am talking vast riches from every corner of the world. Artifacts that the Night Bazaar couldn't even imagine." He stepped closer. "And deep, deep within this cave full of power with riches that would make any sultan look poor is said to be a lamp in which a genie lives. A powerful genie who can grant its master any wish in the world."

A magic lamp? Wasn't that what Mukhtar said he had in his shop? He had been kidding, but even so, Aladdin didn't believe genies were real, especially not genies that granted wishes! Regardless, he let Nasir keep talking.

"Once, long ago, this genie who lives in an itty, bitty living space, granted three wishes that gave the Azalam all the power in the world," Nasir continued, and Aladdin paused.

The Azalam. The ones who had taken his parents. He'd suspected the grand vizier was one of them. Now he knew for sure. Still, he needed to drag things out. "You're part of the Azalam?"

"In a matter of speaking," Nasir said lazily, looking at his own necklace. "The Azalam reigned over all the land for a while, but the magick of the Cave did not like that. Power unchecked, so it said, was no good for man, so a group of sorcerers who claimed to be the guardians of the Cave, cast a spell to hide it from view. The Azalam could no longer access the riches. They had run out of wishes from the genie and later found out the lamp had been stolen by the sorcerers and placed deep inside the Cave. These sorcerers' goal was to correct the balance of power." His eyes narrowed. "They died for that mistake. But still, the job had been done. The beetle that opened the Cave was lost and split in two to keep anyone from single-handedly opening the Cave on their own again."

Two halves of a beetle. Aladdin's grip on his necklace tightened. Heat was pulsing off the charm now. Aladdin felt his body slowly being pulled forward. The beetle wanted to be reunited badly, whether it was meant to do so or not. The whispers were growing even louder, but they were different from the charm's. The voice in Aladdin's head didn't seem to want the two halves of the charm to reunite.

Did he trust the voice in his head or the charm?

And who were his parents if they possessed part of a charm that was used to open up a cave with a magic genie and all the wonders of the world? The questions were overwhelming.

"The sorcerers vowed to protect the Cave at all costs," Nasir continued. "They hid it from the Azalam for centuries, until my own family, loyal members of the Azalam, finally tracked down my half of the beetle." He flashed his necklace again. "We were rewarded with riches, but nothing like the Cave could give us. The Azalam entrusted my family to find the other half of the beetle, and now, I have. Soon, I'll rule the world!" He pressed his fist into the night sky.

"Squawk!" said the bird. "You mean your brother can rule the world."

Nasir's face flamed. "Yes, yes, my brother. Because he's older by eighteen months. As if birthright alone means one would be a better ruler. . . ." He cleared his throat. "But no matter. That other half of the beetle longs to be reunited with mine and my destiny is to bring the pieces together and reopen the Cave. I don't need a future-casting potion to know what's in front of me."

Aladdin paled.

"I must fulfill my destiny. For my brother. For my family. For the Azalam. And then my name will be remembered for all time!"

"Squawk!" said the bird again. "You mean your brother's."

"Enough, Iago!" Nasir barked. He glided toward Aladdin. "That's why you will give the charm to me. It is not yours to keep."

Don't do it, Aladdin! the voice said. Aladdin tripped over his own feet, trying to move away, but something was holding him in place as Nasir reached out a hand to grab the charm from around his neck.

"Don't fight it, boy. This is your destiny as much as it is mine. Don't you see? You were meant to be here, in this time, in this place, in Agrabah, to hand the charm over to me!" His smile brightened. "You, a lowly street rat, being part of a moment that will be remembered forever!"

Aladdin's mouth felt dry. The voice was insistent: *Don't give up the beetle!* And yet, what choice did he have? He looked over at Abu. The monkey was starting to get up. He looked at Aladdin, then at the kids, and headed toward them. If Abu could free his friends, maybe — just maybe — they could all make a run for it. It was a long shot, but he had to keep Nasir distracted.

"I like the idea of being remembered," Aladdin said. "So how do I fit into all this? How did my family come to possess the charm in the first place?" He shrugged. "I am just a nomad."

"Ah, yes," Nasir said, the excitement in his voice rising. "You raise a good point. It seems the sorcerers were smarter than I realized — hiding such a treasure among a people we'd never think to search. We spent years hunting down every silly sultan and rich man, searching their treasures for the other half of the charm, and yet that half of the beetle was resting with a boy who is nothing more than a street rat. The sorcerers knew we'd never look at nomads!"

Aladdin's heart beat faster. "Then how'd you know the charm was in Agrabah?"

Abu had made it to one of the scorpion's legs and was holding a rock. It wasn't much, but maybe if he threw it hard enough, the scorpion would move an inch or two and his friends could untie themselves and . . . and . . . and would be able to slip away. It was a big if, but it was the only shot they had.

"I used a spell," Nasir hissed, sounding much like a snake. "It told me that Agrabah was the key to finding the other half of the beetle. What I didn't know until I was here, and learned of your note obtained at the Night Bazaar, was that I needed more than your charm to open the cave — I needed a Diamond."

Diamond. Aladdin's heart started to drum faster and faster, his lips dry. He tried to steady himself. He'd heard the word *diamond* used only in Agrabah. It was in the voices in his head, in the Night Bazaar, spoken by even Mukhtar. *The Diamond in the rough is near.* Was the charm a diamond?

Or was he . . . the Diamond?

No.

Him? Tasked with watching over a cave he didn't even know existed? It sounded impossible and yet . . .

Could this be why his parents disappeared all those years ago? Were they Diamonds, too? Had the Azalam found them? And did his parents leave Aladdin behind to protect him and throw the Azalam off his trail? He'd never know for sure, but he now knew one thing — this beetle was in his possession because his parents knew he'd protect it. He wasn't just a lowly street rat. He was a Diamond who had carried a charm around his neck for years and survived.

"Apparently only a Diamond can open the Cave with both halves of this charm. So first, you will give me your charm and then we'll see — do I need you to open the Cave or will your guardian come to do it for you?"

"Guardian?" Did Nasir mean Elham? But she was nowhere to be found. What was he going to do?

"Stop stalling! Give me the charm, boy!" The grand vizier flicked his wrist, and the scorpion came to life again. Aladdin's friends awoke, too, their terrified screams echoing through the quiet night. Abu narrowly missed being stabbed by one of the scorpion's legs. The sand pulled him down, sucking him under the scorpion's legs and trapping him with the others.

"NO!" Aladdin yelled.

He was going to lose Abu now, too. His friends needed him. They were his family now and he was their only hope. Aladdin had no choice. *I'm sorry*, he said, thinking of his parents and all the sorcerers before him who had done what he'd failed to do — protect the Diamond that opened the Cave of Wonders. *I don't have a choice. I have to save them.*

Aladdin stepped forward to hand over the necklace and there was a pop and then a bang rocked the earth beneath their feet, knocking them all off-balance. Smoke rose around them and then faded just as fast, revealing a tall man standing between Aladdin and the grand vizier.

"Forget the boy, Nasir."

Aladdin gasped. "Mukhtar?"

Mukhtar didn't answer him. His eyes were on Nasir. "You need a Diamond, do you not?"

Aladdin didn't understand, but Nasir and Iago looked at each other and laughed. "Are we to believe the man who can open the Cave is you?"

Mukhtar stood his ground. "Yes. *I* am the Diamond in the rough."

TWENTY-TWO

MUKHTARISM NUMBER 37:
YOU ARE WORTH MORE
THAN OTHERS THINK YOU ARE.

Aladdin couldn't believe what he was seeing or hearing. Mukhtar was here! In the middle of the desert! Standing between him and the grand vizier! And he was claiming to be the Diamond in the rough?

"Mukhtar, no! You don't understand." Aladdin tried butting in. "The grand vizier has been searching for my charm. Only a Diamond can possess it. That's me. I didn't know that, but I did know my charm could glow. That it seems to talk to me. I guess that's why you wanted me to protect it. You knew the truth." He swallowed hard. "Well, not all of it." He looked down. "I didn't tell you that I ran into the grand vizier that night in the Night Bazaar and he saw my charm. If I had just been honest, this wouldn't have happened."

"It's all right, kid," Mukhtar said quietly. "I wasn't completely honest with you, either, but I'm here now. Let me handle this." He turned back to Nasir. "I am the true Diamond. The kid was covering for me. Now I'm here and I'm prepared to do what others before me failed to do."

Nasir hesitated, looking from Aladdin to Mukhtar. "You're going to open the Cave for me?"

"Well, I can open it for me and then you can tell me what you want me to gather for you," Mukhtar explained. "Only a Diamond can open the Cave, but you know that. I am the Diamond. It is a role I have played since I was a child myself. As I grew, I was meant to be a protector of other, younger Diamonds like Aladdin here." He put a hand on Aladdin's shoulder. "He was meant to be my charge, but I lost him before I even had a chance to train him in how to escape the likes of you."

"What?" Aladdin whispered.

"You were meant to be delivered to me as a kid, Al. I was supposed to keep you safe," Mukhtar said regretfully. "Your parents knew the Azalam were after them. They wanted me to pick you up at a meeting point, but I refused to leave the safety of Agrabah. I told them to deliver you to me." The look in his eyes was pained. "When you never arrived. I searched for you, but it was as if you'd vanished. I fell into despair. I thought I failed you. After that, I stopped training. I set up shop in Agrabah and tried to forget my role as the Diamond." He stared at Aladdin thoughtfully. "I thought you were dead, but then you showed up twelve years later, long after I'd given up hope of finding you. And you had the charm only few in a lifetime are blessed to carry, but you had no clue what it was." He swallowed hard, looking miserable. "I foolishly thought it was better to keep you in the dark."

Aladdin's skin prickled. "Why didn't you tell me?"

Mukhtar grimaced. "I'm sorry, Al. I was thinking with my head, not my heart."

Aladdin closed his eyes for a moment, trying to absorb what he now knew. He was a Diamond. He'd been tasked with protecting the Cave of Wonders. "How could you lie to me? I don't even know how to protect the Cave," Aladdin whispered. "We're doomed." Mukhtar hung his head.

Nasir laughed. "Foolish boy. Don't you know by now? Never trust anyone." He flicked his wrist and Mukhtar flew toward the scorpion, who aggressively stepped over the man, trapping him with the others.

Mukhtar! Aladdin's stomach twisted into a ball of knots. Never trust anyone. That just wasn't true. Mukhtar had still taken him in, given him a job, entrusted him to go to the Night Bazaar. He was special. Aladdin knew that. He was a Diamond. He looked at Mukhtar again and wondered — if Mukhtar had known who he was the whole time, then hadn't he been protecting him, too? Was he protecting Aladdin even now by claiming to be needed to open the Cave?

Think with your head, not your heart. That was Mukhtarism number fourteen. Was his boss trying to tell him something? Aladdin's heart soared. Was he trying to trick the grand vizier? And if he was, was he trying to get Aladdin to do the same?

Aladdin couldn't care less about protecting the wonders in some cave, but his parents had sworn to it, so now it was his duty, too. Mukhtar was tasked with the same responsibility. And to carry it out, he had to outsmart the smartest sorcerer around. Mukhtar had to know whether or not it was true that a Diamond needed to open the Cave. He'd offered to do it himself. Maybe Aladdin could do the same and then . . . he wasn't sure. Did he tell this cave not to give him any riches? Warn the cave about the Azalam? Where was the cave anyway?

Aladdin took a deep breath. An all-powerful Nasir in possession of all those riches and a genie would be a dangerous thing. Aladdin had an idea, but it was risky. Still, it was his only shot. He had dozens of Mukhtarisms at his disposal. He just had to think on his toes and hope the grand vizier's greed got the best of him.

"Wait! Didn't you need Mukhtar to open the cave?" Aladdin asked.

Nasir waved his arm dismissively. "He's too old to travel through a cave that vast and get me what I need." His eyes flashed. "You will have to do instead. Even if you are untrained."

"But I don't know how to get around in this cave. I don't even know what to look for," Aladdin tried. "Remember what you said? I'm a street rat. I don't know a jewel from a . . . rock. Only someone as rich and as brilliant as you could truly get all the wonders they're looking for." He smiled. "Seems to me like *you're* the true Diamond."

"Al, what are you saying?" Mukhtar cried out.

"Quiet!" Nasir scratched his chin. "Yes, I am quite valuable. And I do have the charm."

"You do." Aladdin nodded. "You're rich and you are about to have the full beetle charm. Kind of feels like you're the one meant to open this Cave of Wonders. Plus, I don't know the spells needed to open the Cave."

"Spells?" Nasir's smile faded.

"Yes, summoning spells . . ." Aladdin tried. "The ones used to find the Cave. You know about those, right? Do you see a cave around here?" He looked around. "I don't."

Nasir was quiet.

Aladdin kept going. "You need powerful spells . . . ones only a sorcerer would know. Mukhtar's obviously washed up and can't remember them, and I don't know a thing." He glanced at the macaw. "But maybe this brother the bird keeps yapping about would know a spell to open the Cave."

Nasir's face darkened. "I don't need my brother! I can do a spell myself!"

"You can?" Aladdin pretended to ponder this. "I don't know . . . the talking bird seems to think otherwise. Didn't he say your brother is more powerful or something?" Nasir's face reddened.

"*Squawk!* Did not!"

"Definitely more powerful and probably more handsome, too," Aladdin added for good measure.

"Absolutely not!" Nasir roared. "I can open the Cave myself! My spells are the most powerful in the land! All I need is that charm and then I'll truly be a Diamond!"

"Then take it, Diamond!" Aladdin said, tossing the charm to him.

"Al, no!" Mukhtar cried.

Nasir held the charm up to the sky, a mix of delirium and pleasure written on his face. "Yes! Yes! I've done it! I have the power!" he cried out as the bird squawked by his side. "The Cave of Wonders will soon be mine!"

"Well, it will be your brother's! *Squawk!* Right, Nasir? Nasir?" Iago squawked.

But Nasir was a man possessed. Aladdin watched in wonder as he ripped the beetle from Aladdin's chain and pulled his own necklace off his neck. He held both pieces of the beetle in front of him, and Aladdin watched as the pieces flew together.

SMACK! The halves of the beetle fused as one, glowing bright and seemingly coming alive in front of their very eyes, tiny wings fluttering like magic. The beetle lifted out of Nasir's hands, then took off like a shot, shooting yards away across the desert, leaving a blaze of gold-and-red sparkles in its wake.

"*Squawk!* It wants us to follow it to the Cave!" the bird cried.

Aladdin's heart plummeted. He didn't think the Cave would actually appear if Nasir wasn't a Diamond. He'd just been stalling. But he had to have faith. Be strong. Trust his gut. Nasir was not a Diamond. He wouldn't be able to open the Cave.

"Follow that beetle!" Nasir cried, and with a flick of his wrist, Aladdin went flying backward, where he was caught under the scorpion's legs. Its pinchers were dangerously close to the top of his head. Mukhtar pulled him into the middle of the scorpion with the others.

"Why'd you give Nasir your charm, Al? Why?"

Aladdin had had the wind knocked out of him, but he managed a smile. "It's like you taught me: When in doubt, improvise."

TWENTY-THREE

NASIR

"*Squawk!* Nasir, what are you doing?" Iago flapped his wings in front of the grand vizier. "You have to call for your brother before you try to open that cave! Nasir? He's the more powerful sorcerer! He may know the spell! If anyone was a Diamond, it had to be him. Hello? Nasir?"

But Nasir wasn't listening to his brother's stupid bird. He'd taken the horse and was galloping after the flying beetle, not wanting to let the glittering path out of his sight. Maybe it was his brother's birthright to open the Cave of Wonders. And maybe Nasir did promise to hand over the charm to his brother once he found the other half, but now he saw things differently.

Why hand over the power when it could be his? All his!

He was a powerful sorcerer! The boy said he needed some spell? He knew plenty of spells! Why wait for his brother to appear and try to out-spell him? Nasir could do this himself. He was a Diamond, after all. The kid was right. Now his brooding brother wouldn't be sultan or ruler of the world — *Nasir* would be! It was too delicious a thought to ignore!

Nasir could hear Iago squawking in his ears and the last dying breaths of those worthless street rats and past-his-prime Diamond, but he didn't care. Yes, maybe the older one had been a Diamond once upon a time. He radiated the same energy the boy did. Maybe it was the man's energy that had caused Nasir to come to Agrabah in the first place. Or maybe it was the boy's energy. No matter now. Both Diamonds were in Agrabah and both Diamonds had failed to protect their greatest treasure. Within moments, Nasir would cast a spell and the Cave would open and the wonders within — the lamp! — would be his! All his!

How do you like that, brother? Nasir thought to himself. *You send your younger sibling to do your dirty work and you lose!*

The bird flew in front of him. "*Squawk!* Nasir! Get out of that head of yours! This isn't what is supposed to happen!"

"Of course it is, Iago! Look! Absolute power in my grasp!" Nasir was beyond ecstatic, his eyes growing wider as he watched the beetle. "I am the true Diamond!"

The charm finally stopped, and once more, the pieces separated, the two halves of the charm digging deep into the sand till they resembled two eyes. The dark night sky began to pulse and glow, and then the ground began to rumble beneath their feet like an earthquake. Clouds stormed the sky and lightning flashed. A rumble of thunder actually made Nasir jump, and he realized he'd been so distracted he hadn't thought of a spell yet. The sand was swirling faster and faster now, rising like smoke until it rose as high as a mountain ridge and formed into the shape of a tiger's head with glowing eyes.

The eyes narrowed at Nasir and then its large mouth opened, revealing fangs and and a staircase that led to a brightly lit cavern far below.

"I've found it!" Nasir cried, running toward the cavern. "I've found the Cave of Wonders!"

His steps only slowed as he reached the tiger's gaping mouth. Heat pulsed from the Cave and the light was so bright he could see nothing but a few steps in front of him, steps leading below the tiger's throat. He heard breathing and quickly realized it wasn't his own — it was the tiger's. And look! The Cave wasn't even asking for a spell to open it — it had opened on its own! That foolish street rat had been wrong, after all! He didn't need a spell! Nasir stepped onto the tiger's bottom lip.

A blast of wind from the Cave sent him flying backward.

"Who dares disturb my slumber?" the Cave bellowed.

Slight setback. No matter. He could come up with a good spell. Nasir bowed his head. "It is I, Nasir. Brother of the Azalam, who has long searched for you, Oh powerful Cave of Wonders."

The Cave seemed to think for a moment. "Know this. Only one may enter here. One whose worth lies far within. A Diamond in the rough."

"Nasir! *Squawk!* I don't know about this!"

"Quiet, Iago!" Nasir hissed. *I am a Diamond*, he thought. *I'll even mask myself as that ridiculous boy through a spell. How hard can it be?* Nasir mumbled the changeling spell to himself, saying the words that would make the world view his appearance differently. He focused on that fool Mukhtar and the boy, altering his appearance till he looked as pitiful as a common man like they were. *You want a Diamond?* he thought. *Here's your Diamond!*

He took a step forward. This was his moment!

"I know what I'm doing!" he said, sounding younger, like the boy. He looked down at his street clothes and giggled with glee. Then he walked faster, reaching up for a fang to pull himself up into the tiger's mouth. He paused for a moment. If the Cave suspected he wasn't who he said he was, something would happen right about now.

Nothing did.

Fool, Nasir thought. He was so much more clever than his brother or anyone gave him credit for. *Now let's find that lamp.* Nasir took another step inside, concentrating on the spell that would keep him cloaked as another.

That's when he heard the roar.

The ground began to quake. Iago squawked and flew out of the way. Nasir started to panic, his spell fading before his eyes, leaving him as himself once more.

"Wait!" Nasir cried, looking to grasp something solid as the ground continued to rumble and the fang he'd held on to just moments before started to slip back into sand. "Wait! No!"

He spun around, trying to hold on to the walls that were crumbling around him. If he could just take a few steps, he could jump out of the Cave, but the wind had picked up, pushing him backward. Lightning continued to flash.

Who is the fool now? he thought. The boy had tricked him! Whether the street rat or that old Diamond knew spells or not probably didn't matter. The magic of the Cave was that it knew a true Diamond from a false one, and he was not a true one.

The sand beneath his feet began to slip away and Nasir began to fall, feeling himself pulled deeper and deeper into the Cave.

It occurred to him only at the end that he needed to warn his brother so the same fate didn't befall him. His brother didn't know the Diamond was a person, that it took two things to open the Cave — both the beetle and the person whose worth lay within, as the Cave had said. And now he knew: There was no tricking the Cave of Wonders.

"Jafar!" Nasir tried to cry out as the sand began to swallow his body.

He knew Jafar couldn't hear him, of course. He was too far away, unaware of the true meaning of *the Diamond in the rough*, or what was happening to the beetle's two halves. One of which Nasir had lost once more and one he'd found only to lose again. He was too late.

"I'm so sorry, brother!" Nasir said, flailing to hold on to something before being pulled deeper into the earth. But there was nothing left to hold on to. "I've failed you, Jafar! I've failed — "

Nasir's voice was snuffed out before he could say another word.

TWENTY-FOUR

MUKHTARISM 59:
EVERYONE NEEDS A DAY OFF NOW AND THEN.

Something was happening. Before Aladdin could even try to explain to Mukhtar how he'd tricked the grand vizier, the scorpion towering over them started to waffle and disappear.

"What's going on?" Aladdin cried, scrambling to his feet, taking off running to see where the grand vizier had taken his charm.

"Look!" said Mukhtar, rushing up onto the ridge to see for himself. "The Cave! He's opened it!" He took off running, half tumbling down the ridge of sand, trying to reach the Cave before Nasir entered it.

Opened it? That couldn't be! Didn't one need a Diamond to enter? Aladdin ran, too, racing after Mukhtar, the sand feeling thick and cold as they ran closer and closer to the storm brewing in the middle of the desert. When they'd reached the nearest ridge, Mukhtar stopped short.

"Wait!" he said, putting his arm in front of Aladdin. "Look!"

Aladdin couldn't believe his eyes. The grand vizier appeared to be struggling. They were too far away to hear, but he could see the bird flapping in place near the entrance of what appeared to be a tiger's head made of sand. Thunder and lightning were crashing all around as he heard Nasir cry out in what sounded like terror.

Aladdin finally saw why. The Cave was closing around him! He watched as the entire tiger's head rained down as sand once more, forming itself into a mound of the stuff, taking the grand vizier along with it, but not before there was a loud roar.

"Seek thee out!" Aladdin heard the Cave bellow. "The Diamond in the rough!"

Mukhtar and Aladdin looked at each other in horror. The Cave had swallowed the grand vizier!

Within seconds, all that was left was the two halves of the beetle lying in the sand. Then the night sky brightened once more and all was silent.

Aladdin was speechless. "When I told him to cast a spell, I didn't know that would happen if he lied to get in," he sputtered.

Mukhtar put his arm around the boy. "Mukhtarism number one thousand: Impostors are always found out. So don't be one." He pulled Aladdin into a hug. "I'm glad you're okay, kid. I'm sorry. So sorry."

"No, I'm the one who should be sorry," Aladdin said. "If I'd told you that I'd run into the grand vizier and our charms seemed connected somehow, maybe we could have stopped this from happening."

Mukhtar grasped him by his shoulders. "But you did stop him, kid! You didn't even need my training! You managed to save us all on your own!"

His friends were safe. The grand vizier and his dangerous potions were gone. Aladdin breathed a sigh of relief that quickly turned into a gasp as he saw the bird swoop past him, headed straight for the two halves of the beetle.

"Don't let him get the charms!" Aladdin cried, and he and Mukhtar started running.

The bird was faster, swooping down and grabbing the grand vizier's half of the charm in its beak. It turned back to grab the second half, saw Aladdin and Mukhtar, and flew off into the night. All it left behind was a single red feather.

At least the bird wouldn't have both halves. Aladdin turned back to the sand. "My charm! Where is it?" He began pawing through the sand. "It was just here!" He looked up at Mukhtar. "I don't understand. The bird only got half. The other half was right here! Where did it go?"

"You're talking about sand, kid. There's a lot of it, if you haven't noticed." Mukhtar stood up, dusting off his hands and putting the bird's feather in his pocket. "The only thing that matters is that the macaw only has one piece of the puzzle — he can't open the Cave again without the whole beetle or" — Mukhtar raised his right eyebrow — "a Diamond in the rough. He has neither. The Cave is safe for now. That's what's important."

Aladdin was sad to think he'd lost the only thing he had of his parents, but Mukhtar was right. He'd done his duty — he'd protected the Cave. His parents would be proud. "And at least the grand vizier will never be able to tell anyone what a Diamond actually is."

"Aladdin!" Malik interrupted them. "You're all right! I thought that creepy grand vizier did you in before the scorpion could."

Abu jumped off Malik's back and into Aladdin's arms, chattering loudly. "I'm happy to see you, too, buddy," Aladdin said to the monkey. "Thanks for your help back there."

"Help? I thought the scorpion was going to kill all of us till Mukhtar showed up," Kalila said, throwing her arms around Aladdin. "Why did he want your charm so badly?"

Aladdin paled and looked at Mukhtar. "Uh . . ."

"Yeah! Can someone please explain what is going on?" Fatima demanded. "All this talk of you and Aladdin being Diamonds, as if you're secretly royalty. If that's true, why is Mukhtar's shop full of junk?" She looked at him. "No offense."

"What's important is that Aladdin tried to rescue us," Kalila pointed out, smiling at him. She rubbed Abu's back. "Him and Abu! You guys are heroes!" Abu squeaked happily.

"That is true," Fatima said, and looked at Aladdin. "It was decent of you to almost die trying to save us . . . after being the reason we were captured in the first place since the grand vizier was after you and you didn't warn us! How do you know him anyway?"

Aladdin and Mukhtar looked at each other again. "Uh . . ."

Malik shook his head. "Strangest apology ever."

Aladdin laughed. "I'll still take it."

"I guess that means we should keep you around," Malik added with a smile.

"Sounds good to me," said Kalila.

"Yes, yes, we're reunited, but both of you better spill it!" Fatima said again. "I still don't understand — you're a Diamond? You can do magic? You have powers?"

Mukhtar looked as uncomfortable as Aladdin. "No, neither of us has powers." He looked at Aladdin worriedly. "It's a long story and one I'd rather tell in front of a warm fire with some soup. Let's get home and I'll tell you everything, team."

"And how are we getting there?" Malik asked. "We're pretty far from Agrabah."

Mukhtar motioned to the horse that was still standing nearby that Aladdin had ridden. "Al has a ride and can take one or two of you.

And over that ridge is my horse. It will be tight, but we can get us all back to Agrabah before the night ends."

The group didn't have to be told twice. They trudged through the sand, mounted the horses, and sat uncomfortably with three on one and two on the other to trek back to the city. It felt like a longer journey heading back than it had been going. Of that much Aladdin was sure.

"I don't think I've ever wanted to sleep on the ground more than I do right now," Malik said with a yawn as they reached the last sandy ridge. Beyond it, Agrabah rose up as if to greet them.

The city was still alight, and the music had grown louder, as had the sounds of people cheering and singing inside the city walls, staying up way past normal bedtimes. Aladdin was relieved to know the spell over the city that the grand vizier had cast had dissolved, too.

"I think I will sleep for a week," Kalila agreed.

"Now, now, you guys can take a day or two off to rest after what happened, but we can't go a week without work," Mukhtar piped up.

"Why do we have to work anymore when you can do magick?" Malik asked. "You're this Diamond thing, right? You can just poof up anything we want, right?"

"And we've got two — you *and* Aladdin," Fatima pointed out. "Why don't you start by conjuring something for us to eat. I'm starving!"

Aladdin and the others laughed. They were so busy joking around, they didn't notice the crowd gathered by the city gates or the group of camels packed high with belongings.

"Aladdin!"

Aladdin froze. "Elham?"

He felt as if his heart might burst as he saw a woman rushing toward him. He scrambled to get off the horse and greet her.

"We thought we'd lost you!" Elham said, pulling him into a tight embrace that smelled familiar — like camel hair, cardamom, and that lotion she was always rubbing on her skin. Elham was here! "I didn't think we'd ever see you again! We've been searching the city for days, going from one end to the other asking about you!"

Aladdin looked up at her and smiled. "So you were really looking for me, too? I looked for you everywhere."

"Of course!" Elham looked surprised. "We were frightened when we couldn't find you before the sandstorm. The storm came up so quickly that we had to pack up camp and take shelter inside the city without finding you first. I was so worried."

"It was my fault," Aladdin said. "I walked away from the market to see Agrabah, and by the time I realized how far I'd gotten, the storm was here." He hung his head. "I know everyone always says I have my head in the clouds. Or more like the stars."

She smiled. "What did I always tell you? The stars are there to listen. You're a dreamer, boy. Always have been. Nothing wrong with that."

"So you weren't mad at me for getting lost?"

"Why would I be mad?" Elham asked. "I was concerned. Not mad."

Aladdin had misread everything!

Elham pulled him in tight again. "Oh, sweet boy, did you think we abandoned you?"

Aladdin's face flamed. "Maybe? I waited out the storm and then returned to the Bedouin outside the city, but you were gone. I didn't know what to do." He glanced over at his friends and then at Walid and Yusuf standing awkwardly next to their camels. "My new friends took me in."

Elham smiled. "I'm glad you were safe." She touched his chin. "And I'm thankful we found you. Now we can bring you home."

"Home," Aladdin repeated, thinking of their traveling Bedouin, never staying long in one place, never putting down roots.

"The thought of leaving you behind broke my heart," Elham said. "You're one of us."

One of us. Aladdin appreciated the words. It felt like a weight had been lifted off him to know that Elham cared about him as much as he cared for her. He would forever be grateful that she took him in and cared for him his whole childhood, but now that he knew his parents always wanted him to be with Mukhtar in Agrabah, he knew for certain this city was where he belonged.

Over Elham's head, he could see beyond the city gates through the crowded streets and could just make out the oval-shaped tops of the palace in the distance, where a bored princess was probably ignoring the new-moon dinner going on outside her balcony window.

Agrabah may have been crowded, and loud, and busy, but it was also exciting, beautiful, and full of new adventures. Aladdin felt pulled to this city in a way he hadn't felt anywhere he'd been in his lifetime. For once in his life, he felt like he was exactly where he was supposed to be.

He looked at the woman who was as close to a mother as anyone had been. "I'm so happy you found me, but I think I am going to stay here in Agrabah."

Abu screeched happily.

"Really?" Kalila squealed. "I'm so happy!"

"We'd miss you if you left, Aladdin," Malik added.

"Even I would — a little," Fatima said with a wink. "We wouldn't have made it through today without you." She gave his arm a squeeze.

Kalila came around the other side of him. "You truly always have our back."

Malik walked over and nudged Aladdin's other side. "And we have yours."

Aladdin saw Elham smile even though her eyes were rimmed with tears. "You're practically a young man now. If Agrabah is where you want to call home, then I won't stop you." She looked at the others. "It looks like you've made some good friends in your time here already. Only you know where your heart belongs, Aladdin."

Staring at Abu, his friends, and the city, Aladdin didn't hesitate. "I think I belong here."

Elham nodded. "We're going to miss you, sweet Aladdin. But this isn't goodbye. We will be back through from time to time to check up on you. I can't imagine not seeing you again."

"Same here," Aladdin said, reaching out and hugging her again. "Thank you, Elham, for everything. Take good care of Lina for me," he said, thinking of his favorite camel.

"I will," Elham promised. "And you take care of yourself, too, Aladdin." She cupped his face. "Something tells me you're destined to do great things."

"Me too," Mukhtar said, speaking up. "Someday the city of Agrabah is going to thank its lucky stars that Aladdin lives here."

TWENTY-FIVE

MUKHTARISM NUMBER 42:
YOU CAN'T TRICK A TRICKSTER.

After goodbyes were said, they made their way back to Mukhtar's shop. Sleep should have been the first order of business, but instead, Mukhtar broke out some tea and some cheese he had been saving for a special occasion and the group feasted, trading stories about what they thought just happened in the desert.

"It was a dream," Kalila said.

"A nightmare," Malik corrected.

"Aladdin is a Diamond, and Mukhtar a magick-maker," Fatima said, shaking her head. "I didn't even think magick was real!"

Abu started hopping up and down chattering, and Aladdin knew he was trying to tell the group about the Night Bazaar's magick, too. Thankfully Aladdin was the only one who understood him. But he couldn't wait to talk to Mukhtar about it all now that he could talk — really talk — to someone who knew about his charm, and Diamonds, and real magick. Oh, the things he'd learn with Mukhtar as his teacher!

Mukhtar cleared his throat and looked at Aladdin. "I guess I should explain why I wasn't at the shop when you all got back. I had a feeling someone was after Al and I wanted to be prepared. I left to go to a special bazaar," he said pointedly, and Aladdin knew he meant the Night Bazaar, "where I could buy some potions to aid me in protecting you all. When I returned, and you all weren't there, I knew something had happened. I saw the mist rising from the city, saw everyone under a spell I had escaped by being at the bazaar, and followed it into the desert. That's where I found all of you and the grand vizier going on and on about the Diamond in the rough. You have to understand: I haven't thought of myself as a Diamond in a very long time — not since the time I lost you when you were a baby."

"You knew Aladdin as a baby?" Fatima piped up, but Mukhtar focused on Aladdin.

"I thought I had failed as a Diamond, but I see now fate had a different path for both of us. We weren't destined to meet twelve years ago," Mukhtar told him. "We came together at the right moment, to stop the Azalam from opening the Cave of Wonders."

"The Cave of what?" Kalila asked.

"And we did it — you did it," Mukhtar clarified. "Without even any Diamond training! Which makes me wonder . . . maybe it is time all Diamonds carved out a new path for themselves."

"Anyone else think Mukhtar is ignoring us?" Malik joked.

Aladdin frowned. "What do you mean?"

Mukhtar looked at him. "Maybe Diamonds going forward shouldn't know who they truly are. Maybe they should be kept in the dark and kept safe. You were safe till you knew the truth, weren't you? If you hadn't known you were a Diamond, and no one else knew, then you *and* the Cave would have been protected." He tapped his chin. "Yes. That gives me an idea."

"Can someone explain what you're talking about?" Fatima tried again.

"But I already know I'm a Diamond! Now you can train me," Aladdin tried, but Mukhtar was already grabbing a small gold lamp from a bookcase.

"I'll explain everything with the help of this," he said.

"Is that the magic lamp from the Cave of Wonders that Nasir was looking for?" Aladdin asked, confused.

"Nope," Mukhtar said. "That one is still safe in the Cave. This is a different one."

"Wow! You mean magick lamps are real?" Malik rushed over to look at the lamp.

"You have a genie at your service and you never told us?" Kalila gasped.

"Can we use him for wishes, too?" Fatima reached out her hand to brush the lamp.

Mukhtar gently pulled the lamp away. "This lamp is real, I swear! And what's better, I'm going to let us all make a wish at the same time and everyone's wish will be granted."

"Really?" Aladdin asked, and Mukhtar nodded. "Is that such a good idea? I mean, are Diamonds allowed to do that? Aren't there rules to magick like there are to being part of your team?"

Mukhtar smiled at him. "Hands in, team. I'll tell you everything later. Right now, we wish," Mukhtar said, placing his hand on the lamp and closing his eyes. "Everyone do like me and I'll tell you when to make your wish."

"What are you going to wish for?" Kalila asked Aladdin.

"I don't know," he admitted. He had kind of gotten everything he'd wanted when he was invited to stay with them. But he felt funny saying that. What he really wanted was to talk to Mukhtar more about being a Diamond.

"I'm wishing that we finally have the funds to get a bigger place and I can get my own room," said Fatima. "You all snore."

"I want enough food to last us a year. No, two years. No, ten years!" Malik said.

"Some new clothes," Kalila said dreamily. "Or some bracelets I could actually keep." They all laughed.

"Ready, Al?" Mukhtar asked.

Everyone, including Abu, reached their hand in to touch the lamp.

Aladdin still hesitated. Something felt off about all this. Mukhtar had hidden his gift as a Diamond and now he was using it in the open?

"Hands in, Al," Mukhtar said again. "And close your eyes."

They all closed their eyes. Okay, half closed. Aladdin couldn't help but peek. That's how he noticed Mukhtar whispering. The lamp started to glow just like the beetle, and Aladdin gasped. The glow brightened till the whole shop was awash in red and gold that looked a lot like fireflies. The other kids' and Abu's eyes were closed tight in concentration, almost as if they were in a trance, but Aladdin was wide-awake

"Let them forget, for now isn't the time to remember — all of them, including the grand vizier's macaw," he heard Mukhtar say. "Someday the Diamond will be needed to stop a threat even bigger than this one. Until that time, let them all forget about the Diamond in the rough."

"Forget?" Aladdin protested, and Mukhtar looked at him. "No, Mukhtar, I want to remember everything that happened! I have so much to learn!"

Mukhtar smiled. "You will learn it all, Al. When the time is right."

"Now's the time!" Aladdin tried, but Mukhtar was already lost again in concentration, closing his eyes and saying a few other things Aladdin didn't understand.

Wait! Aladdin wanted to cry out again, but it was already too late. The glow started to pulse, the lamp started to fade away, and before Aladdin knew it, the world had faded to black.

EPILOGUE

MUKHTARISM NUMBER 77:
THERE IS NO "I" IN TEAM.

The next thing Aladdin knew, it was morning. Sunlight streamed through the slats of the door and his friends were starting to stir. The sound of Mukhtar thundering around above them was a comforting one and Aladdin stared at the wooden stars carved into the beams. Funny how he'd forgotten they were there. And he couldn't remember anything about the night before.

Fatima yawned. "That must have been some new-moon dinner. I feel like I've been asleep for days!"

"Me too," said Malik. "I can't even remember what we did at the dinner party."

"Neither can I," Kalila said.

Abu squeaked, and Aladdin felt the same way. "We must have gone to the festivities, but I don't remember anything we did."

"That's because you all overloaded on fun!" said Mukhtar, stepping down into the shop and looking at Aladdin. "And some of you helped save the city."

"From what? Food poisoning?" asked Malik.

The kids laughed, but Aladdin felt a prickling at the back of his neck that told him Mukhtar wasn't joking. Aladdin might not have remembered what happened the night before, but something told him that night had been magical. The only thing he remembered was saying goodbye to Elham. It made him sad to say goodbye but excited, too — Agrabah was where he belonged and no matter what happened, this city was the one he knew he would always call home.

"All right, everyone clean up and get ready! We've got some magick to find!" Mukhtar told them.

"What routine do we want to try today?" Fatima asked the others. "Something new? Monkey for sale?"

Abu chattered in annoyance.

"She's just kidding," Kalila said with a laugh. "But I do think you could help with some tricks — maybe people would be so distracted watching you perform that the rest of us could get ahold of some worthy goods."

"That's the thinking, team," Mukhtar boomed. He motioned to Aladdin. "Can I talk to you for a minute outside, Al?"

Aladdin startled. Had he done something wrong? "Sure."

Stepping into the alleyway with Mukhtar, he was surprised to feel the man clap him on the back. "Listen, there is something I should have told you when we met a week ago, but I wasn't sure how to explain. Still, I think you deserve to know the truth about your past."

"What is it?" Aladdin asked, curious.

Mukhtar hesitated. "It's about your parents."

"My parents?" Aladdin said in surprise. "You knew them?"

"In a matter of speaking," Mukhtar said, running a hand through his hair. "When you were a babe, they were in danger and knew it. Someone got word to me that I needed to take in a baby, and I believe that baby was you, but then you never showed up. That was twelve years ago. The minute I saw you last week, let's just say I got a strange feeling you were that baby."

Aladdin didn't understand. "How do you know for sure?"

"You had this necklace they gave you," Mukhtar said. "You lost it at the festival yesterday. You were really upset about it, too."

"Necklace?" For some reason, Aladdin couldn't remember having a necklace. But he remembered knowing somehow his parents loved him more than anything. Maybe it was the voice he always heard in his head, pushing him forward, telling him to do good in the world. It sounded silly, but he liked to think it was his mother and father, watching over him in some way. "I lost it?"

"Yes, but you'll never lose your parents' love," Mukhtar said, his voice gruff. "I know they wouldn't have left you if they didn't think it was the only way to save you." He placed a hand on Aladdin's shoulder. "They loved you enough to give you a better life, even if it took some unexpected twists and turns to get here. One thing I do know, kid: You were meant to come to Agrabah. Your journey is only starting."

"Thanks, Mukhtar. I believe that," Aladdin said.

The door creaked and Abu popped his head out of the shop. He started to whine.

"What is it, buddy?" Aladdin asked.

Abu reached under his hat and pulled out a jeweled ring. Aladdin recognized it immediately.

"Is that the grand vizier's?" He looked at Mukhtar. "I met him . . . I think . . . somewhere." The details were foggy, but he could swear he'd crossed paths with the man. Why else would he remember this ring? It was missing a stone, though.

"If you mean Nasir, that guy is gone," Mukhtar said. "I heard the Sultan is already looking for a replacement."

"What happened to him?" Aladdin wondered. "Didn't he just start the job a week ago?"

Mukhtar shrugged. "Someone said he got caught in a sandstorm."

He took the ring from Abu. "But this is quite the catch, no matter whose it is. Nice jewel! Do you know what this thing is worth? Why it's enough to . . ." Mukhtar stopped talking, looking embarrassed.

"Enough to what?" Aladdin wondered, and Abu leaned in to hear.

"Take a long-awaited journey," Mukhtar said. "Can I let you in on a little secret? I know the kids don't believe this magick stuff, but it's true. My family has long been in the business of finding magick artifacts and protecting them, as it were. And for a long time, I've heard about this city near the sea — Ezra's Oasis — that has more magick in it than anywhere near Agrabah." He rubbed his chin. "I've long wondered if it's true but have never had the extra funds to go see for myself. With this ring, I could."

"Ezra's Oasis," Aladdin repeated. "That sounds both exciting and dangerous."

Mukhtar shrugged. "What's a little adventure without some danger? But I could use a sidekick. The other kids can watch the shop — we won't be gone forever. I don't think any of them would really know what to do if real magick came calling. Something tells me, though, that you just might." He held out his hand.

Go, Aladdin, the voice in his head said.

Maybe it was his conscience, maybe it was his parents, but either way, Aladdin knew the voice was right. "An adventure? Involving magick? I'm in!" He reached for Mukhtar's hand and shook it.

Whoosh! A burst of images flooded his mind — one involving a bored princess in the palace, a genie, and him becoming a prince? That didn't make sense, but it sure was a nice fantasy. He pulled his hand away and looked at Mukhtar.

Mukhtar smiled. "Something wrong?"

"No," Aladdin answered. He had an exciting adventure on the horizon and a city at his feet brimming with possibilities. There was no need to fantasize. Life was happening right now. "Everything is just right."

ACKNOWLEDGMENTS

Getting to create a whole new world (pun definitely intended) for Aladdin at age twelve was almost too much fun to be called work! Special thanks goes to series creator Jocelyn Davies for the brainstorming sessions we had discussing the Cave of Wonders, Abu, and the benefits of magic carpet rides and to editor extraordinaire Regan Winter who has taken the reins of the Lost Legends series and helped me fine-tune Aladdin's story. I'm so thankful to have a friend in you both. (You guys see what I did there, right?)

The entire team at Disney has been incredible getting the word out about the Lost Legends during an unusual two years. I'm so thankful to the artistic talents of illustrator Erwin Madrid and designer Phil Buchanan for this eye-popping Aladdin cover, and to the entire team at Disney Books including Ann Day, Augusta Harris, Holly Rice, Dina Sherman, Cassidy Leyendecker, Jody Corbett, and Sharon Krinsky for all you've done to infuse Disney magic into these books. Special thanks also goes to Shazia Mian and Rhonda Ragab at SILA Consulting for all their notes and helpful suggestions.

To my agent, Dan Mandel, thanks for being my magic genie and for always taking my ideas to new heights. And to my Disney-loving writer friends — Mari Mancusi, Tiffany Schmidt, and Lindsay Currie — who are always up for a Disney movie discussion session: I couldn't have done this book without you.

Finally, to my Disney-loving family — my husband Mike and two boys, Tyler and Dylan — who like to discuss Disney Park rides, share Disney TikToks, and want to talk about wait times for WDW and Disneyland rides even when we're at the dining room table: There is no one I'd rather be on this magic carpet ride with.